Blood On Her Hands

Romney B Duffey

PAPERBACK: ISBN: 978-1-966876-79-3

Contents

Chapter 1

Russian Roulette

Early morning with a cold warning

The sun rose quietly as a golden orb casting a red glare and glow over the minarets of St Basils' Cathedral in Red Square, cutting shadows and glistening on the snowy roofs. The lines of traffic were already clogging the streets, drivers weaving from one lane to another in hope of moving.

Even in this cold, during the day she wore the cloth as if sprayed onto her flesh, so tight that every fold and crease of the pant legs revealed the moves and strides she made beneath. The heels on the boots were high and spiked, to dig into the snow or ice. The fur that wrapped the skin was curled and frothy, just like her laughter.

Few knew, but during the night she wore little at all, the cloth designed to bare the skin, to seduce the eyes and entrap the hands. Thin straps of lace, thin wisps of silk, thinly disguised the body beneath.

During the day he always wore a suit, tight buttoned, cut close, in the style of business, with a tie and layers of overcoat to keep out the bitter, seeking wind. His shirts were tailored, tucked and too expensive.

Few knew that during the night, as he looked at her, he wore little at all, loins clothed in silk and hands always reaching out for her...

Arnika rose and peered into the dawn light sweeping across the street as she moved slowly to the window. Already the traffic was six lanes wide, choking the road and the air with exhausts and driver exhaustion.

"I must go now," stated Arnika.

"Why now?"

"You know why."

And he did. He held her tightly, smoothing her, and she responded with kisses and a smile.

Yet she dressed quickly, the apartment her salon, the kitchen a coffee house, the door a locked entry to many secrets.

"See you later," and she was gone, crossing the traffic that blocked the intersection with assured steps, following the crowd into the underpass, knowing his eyes were on her still.

The tall building loomed like a castle.

The guard stood chilled and grey and barely looked as she passed. As always, the security screening was slow and tortured- shedding the coat, the bag, the belt, passing the breathing machines, the portals and the stares at her beauty Then reclaiming what was lost and squeezing into the elevator with the others whose grey lives were already lost in the routine of another day.

The corridors seemed endless, the life drawn from them. Endless rooms after rooms, until the door marked "конференция". In that room, uniformed guards again, and the water glasses laid around the endless wooden table with empty chairs in ranks like solitary sentinels.

"Arnika, my love, how are you?" Half-hidden by his morning beard shadow, Director Orlov looked pale, despite the false color in his cheeks. It was early enough that the vodka had not yet left his body. "Where have you been?"

Such a simple question- such a complicated answer.

"Nowhere much- I was at the UN Conference, and it took an age to get a flight out of New York. There was a storm, a big one. They give them double names, like Jo-Jo, and hurricane winds and rain come more often now the climate has changed." Her voice trailed off, but he looked for more. "There was a lot of talk about the environment, about oil and gas, about the price, and who would pay what to who to stop producing."

"We will all pay."

"Yes, but some will pay more than others."

"As my very special advisor, I expect you to continue to take very, very great care of us, Arnika, and of our interests and what we pay!"

The threat was real, the meaning clear, so all she could do was smile as she sat down amongst the water glasses.

They chatted about what she had heard and found out: the claim to keep the earth cool by paying people for not using carbon fuels. It was a gigantic and politically motivated 'shell game' that did not actually reduce the use of carbon fuels like coal, oil and gas but allowed it by issuing quotas of emissions permits under international treaties and with bureaucratic United Nations agreement. The whole scheme used funds from the "Green Deal Treaty Banks," known behind the scenes by their acronym the "GREEDY Banks." Arnika explained how the rich investors could now get even richer by selling and trading in the allocated carbon permits, rights and credits that allowed those who needed to just continue emitting, all subsidized by guarantees.

Director Orlov asked: "What did you find out about this man named Hsu? Is he for real? Have we met him before somewhere? I am curious, especially about someone who we know little about."

"Yes, he is real- the deal and the money are there but it is dangerous." Arnika paused. "There is something else going on behind the carbon trades, but I do not know what it is yet. Let's get him in here and see what the deal is."

The door was opened again by a guard, and the 'Agent' walked in, his tight-buttoned suit a little looser than Orlov's, his hair falling casually, his tie a pink flower in the daylight streaming through the skylights.

He was calling himself Clifford Hsu, an Asian-American mix, no trace of an accent, shaking hands and trading business cards, and briefly eying Arnika's curves.

Making an offer

Some preliminary remarks, some small talk, some pouring of coffee and tea by a brand new guard who carried it like champagne

"Let's get down to business," Orlov pronounced solemnly, and turned towards Hsu, who was already pulling papers from his shoulder bag and then passing them around. Hsu began slowly to make sure the words counted, moving to the end of the table with a screen and an old-fashioned projector.

"These are the draft contracts. As you are already aware, I act as the sole directed Agent representing major interests in oil, gas and nuclear energy and in emissions credits- they may be known to you as Energy Asset Inc., or EAI."

He paused to make sure he had Orlov's full attention. "As their Agent, we have a special proposition for you that is likely to be of mutual importance and benefit. My talk is on some slides, which are in the handouts. This is indeed a formal proposition but confidential, of course."

Hsu smiled fleetingly, and then the slides whizzed across the screen like cards in a magician's hands.

"The investment would be just five billion from your enterprise, known to the world as Energoatomgazprom and its affiliates." Then, now looking directly at Orlov, Clifford added still more charm for emphasis.

"The deal is really quite simple: we sell energy as oil, gas and uranium to those who need to trade in carbon taxes and credits but have no supplies. The so-called developing nations need to show they are helping and making some reduction in emissions – at least on paper so they can get even more subsidies and loans from the rich nations. You know, all the "Net Zero," "Emissions Avoidance," "Green Credits," and "Carbon Offset", all the fashionable buzz words used by the climate change folks today. But it is all factually underwritten and funded by the usual EU governments and trading subsidies from their central banks."

The slides now became more complex, covered in diagrams of countries, with arrows showing energy flows, and lines showing pipelines zigzagging like ladders across Europe. Hsu knew the international energy and euro-scene well, so placed it all in context, emphasizing each point.

"We believe that Europe will pay top price for carbon credit rights because they have no oil and gas to trade, but the economy still needs the energy. So they must use fuel. They also want to show they are environmentally friendly and are definitely committed to trading in these carbon credit and offset schemes. It is simply to make the Eurocrats in Brussels look good and eco-friendly while really doing nothing: great for image-polishing and influencer interviews."

A deal is a deal

Orlov nodded but was in no mood to hear what he already knew. "So, what is *my* deal?"

 Hsu knew he had him interested and quickened his pace. "The offsets, the credits, will come from your Russian new and recycled uranium fuel that you make and ship for your nuclear plants in Turkey, Egypt, Iran, India, South Africa and China. Now."

He pointed at Orlov for emphasis. "Did you know you can get even more credits if you ship it back for re-cycling and re-processing using my trading company, EAI? The deal is the huge carbon reduction amounts are verified by us as being real, and are registered as exchangeable 'credits' that constitute our joint equity."

Here Agent Hsu paused. "Your share or cut is fifty-fifty with EAI on whatever profit is made on the carbon credit trades. The funds can be transferred or used through accounts you designate in Moscow...." He smiled cynically, "I understand they already look after your pension funds very well."

Hsu elaborated, "To control the assets we, EAI and your designated entity, will form a Joint Venture, including the interest from others, in particular China Energy Corp, with whom we are also affiliated. The bottom line could be a profit of several hundred percent, provided the customer—if it is contracted to be the EU - is paying in euros or convertible currency."

Arnika sat quietly watching Orlov's reactions, just smiling or nodding occasionally. Orlov was both a clever and ruthless person, rising to the top of the political ladder, step by slippery step. He knew not to show how he really felt so remained impassive, almost detached, outwardly calm.

But Hsu knew Orlov was interested- there was no shuffling, no pouring of gassy water into glasses, no interruptions. He continued with the sales pitch.

Pressing on, he emphasized: "In a nutshell, just as you have planned for so long, border and ethnic wars aside, Europe is now at your and China's mercy for their long-term energy supply, especially as any alternative oil and gas pipelines are through Ukraine and Turkey, the Baltic and the Crimea - regions you can easily control."

Hsu paused again: "But you know all this already from your own agents and intelligence. Your deliberate government strategy is to keep your customers dependent on you both for energy and fuel. You can even threaten to increase their gas supply prices. Am I right?"

Orlov nodded and leant forward, thinking.

"And what about the USA?" Orlov asked at last, with a slight smile adding, "Can they be a problem?"

There was a flicker of a smile, a giveaway of concern for his adopted home country as Hsu showed he knew the realities of geopolitics.

"They have their own raft of problems- trade deficits, government deficits, and the assumed role of trying to be the world's policeman enfeebles them. They have lost so much leverage and credibility, with you, with everyone. They focus now on ensuring their own domestic supply and on making profits any way they can. In the USA it is always and only about the money."

Clifford then drove the point home. "The business and energy trade future lies with China. The Chinese have locked up their nuclear fuel supplies in Africa, even now start to make moves in the Pacific. So we must have them in on the deal too. That is where I come in. Both the US and China trust me, as well as you."

"I agree," Arnika's voice was level and strong, and the intervention timed and to add to the punch line. "The USA wheeler-dealers, hedge funds and private investors want to make money, any way they can. They just want to make profits outside the usual regulated trading systems on Wall Street. They will use crypto-currencies and offshore traders so the Federal Reserve, the SEC and the others will never catch up. The Chinese will want to join in- especially if it helps make someone high up the hierarchy very rich."

Hsu saw the effect of the words and the nods of agreement, so continued. "We can make a killing. But I really have more to say and to offer off the record. It is how the deal is structured, the rights divided, the business organized and how, when and where the cash will flow."

He could not resist adding: "Just like environmental emissions, much of what we do and propose must be invisible and difficult to track to its source."

Orlov still displayed no outward reaction. He looked at Arnika, then turning to Hsu. "A deal is a deal. So we must arrange to meet somewhere else - somewhere nice but secure and my banker can be there."

And so she was.

Dinner for four at eight

Olga Petrova was a formidable sight, large and frilled, with a briefcase that would take money stuffed in bundles and never show it. The dinner table lay lit by many small candles, so the shadows flickered under her eyes and accented her high, almost Mongolian cheekbones. But her eyes betrayed nothing beneath the thick eyebrows and the glasses and the calculating mind.

She could count anything, see the money move, manipulate and read the files, program the spreadsheets, foretell the market moves. But one thing she did not see coming later was the knife-cutting her neck. But that was later.

Up-scale was the only description for this restaurant, no expense spared in décor and ambience. They assembled quietly, the Agent, Arnika, the banker and someone half in and half out of the candle's shadows. He looked just like someone from the Eisenstein's Boyers Plot movie, the scraggy pointed beard, the aquiline profile, and the deep piercing eyes. He was Yuri, the Director's designated hit man and dealmaker.

"Let us order a drink and dinner," was Olga's contribution.

"Let's get down to it," was all Yuri said, who had no time for anything that took time.

Arnika flashed him one of her golden smiles, crossed her legs slowly to reveal a hemline just too high to be respectable, and ordered wine and dinner.

Agent Hsu looked cool and relaxed, his suit jacket unbuttoned to reveal a clean, rippling shirt. The deal was being made and seemed so easy now. The dinner was elegant and slow so after the small talk and toasts of friendship finally he broke the ice.

"I have something to add that I could not say today. It's a financial jungle out there- everyone wants to make money. Including us." Hsu now revealed his hidden scheme. "The unstated part of this private deal is the insurance for the cargo and re-insurance of the credits. Basically, we treat the debt or liability as an asset with value, just like the bad real estate loans in the last financial crisis. This ensures our venture against any loss which we can claim if for some unforeseen reason something might happen to it. It could double our profit."

Orlov stopped chewing and drinking. "Oh, you mean some international incident, or some mischief happens, but of course, that could never, ever happen... not with Russia involved." Everyone smiled.

Olga opened the business bidding after several more glasses of wine. "I have the contract in draft here for you to take to your principles- it should be signed and sealed within the month. You understand?"

Clicking off the points one by one, she continued setting up the transaction. "The money- the down payment- should be paid into these numbered accounts that are listed. OK? If these are not working, I have more – it is our official retirement fund. OK? The bank is official, the accounts are official, but in my name. Use encoded transfers."

She handed over several sheets of paper, produced from the depths of the briefcase.

"There is only one problem. OK?" The air was tense suddenly. What problem? "Who will pay for the shipping?"

Olga was looking to squeeze as much cash as possible from the deal. "There are shipments listed in the scope of the contracts, and in the deal you presented. OK? There are shipping charges, insurance, security, costs, inspections, extras...who knows whatever and whoever else has to be paid. So who pays for all that?"

Olga repeated slowly and clearly. "OK? So who pays?"

The Agent looked rather surprised. "The shipping is all in third-party vessels sub-contracted by Russia. There are and should be no separate charges."

Arnika was always a lateral thinker despite her makeup and wardrobe, so feigning too much alcohol intake offered: "We could even call it something else harmless so the cost is less. Everyone does that all the time for shipments of guns, rockets and bombs. Perhaps it all gets lost at sea, just disappears and we collect the insurance. Why not?... I am joking of course ..."

Yuri was also thinking, albeit slowly, about his contribution, and took the offered bait.

"I have contacts in our recycling company and the shipping organizations. We can cover any cost under normal shipments and the insurance will be OK - it will already be disguised and listed as a normal-type shipment ..... If there is any problem we will dump all the cargo overboard–lost at sea means there is no evidence left to inspect and insurers pay up. No one will even want to try to recover the nasty cargo from that wreck. I can make sure of that."

Yuri smiled, adding with a hand wave. "Even the crew may disappear. We can make it all happen."

And so that is how it was to be. Led by Orlov, the deal was sealed with toasts and shots of old high-test vodka.

Sunrise over the palace

They all went their separate ways, slipping into the night shadows, the streets slightly wet from the rain. But as Olga left that evening, happy at the thought of more money flowing, she sensed someone was following her.

She could not be sure, the dark streets, the many people, the headlights shimmering, and even on the subway and the throng of people. Perhaps she was mistaken, perhaps, perhaps not. She quickened her pace slightly.

That night Arnika shed her clothes again in a good cause- and he was very grateful.

The sunrise was gorgeous with the red tones reflecting the colour of the houses and the high walls of the Kremlin, always standing guard. The shadows cast by the buildings cut across the street.

It reminded Arnika of another wondrous city, with its walls and history, but where markets and people still crowded out the traffic. Where the sound of the call to prayers echoed from the towers, the loud speakers vibrating with the chanting words thrown into the air. Glistening across the water, the calls seemingly faded as the sun rose.

Another day of opportunities was springing to life...

Chapter 2

Life and Death in Italy

Bar fly

Tall, elegant in a slightly untidy way, with a slight day's beard growth, he had just caught up on his emails and was sitting down at the bar, when he noticed her.

Perched on a stool, long legs gracefully curled together, tanned skin glistening and hemline just respectably above the knees. The music and chatter were loud, and from the pool came the sounds of glasses and laughter of a wedding party gaining strength,

He had found the hotel arriving late at night from Pisa airport, its line for "All Passports" and the luggage carousel crowded as usual as the tourists scrambled for entry and for their bags. He was just wheeling his whole life in a small carryon.

The flight had been a little delayed, as usual, but the drive to the hotel was direct, without the obligatory glimpse of the leaning tower. He missed its white shining marble companions, in the bustling and truly-named Piazza dei Miracoli.

His miracle was that the rental car was ready, and the rental car lady was also lovely, with a great accent but no maps. Her phone locator was her best offer, so he pulled out his own GPS navigator, entered the address into "where to" and was off. He had been told to meet her at the hotel, but not where. Perhaps this was the place, perhaps this was her.

Perhaps not.

She caught his eye, she knew that. He knew that she knew.

It was later that night, when the sounds had all died away, and the night had wrapped their bodies in warmth, that they really talked. It had seemed so long since the days in the cold.

"We cannot go on meeting like this" was almost an understatement as she turned softly and languorously in the sheets. "It is too dangerous. They will find out."

"I don't care. The world is passing us by, faster and faster, there is no time."

"There is always no time – it is what you do with it that counts."

"Then let us make it count."

"Uno, due, tre....." and her smile broke the count. "I always think we should take much more time out together, but ...we must plan our days carefully, we must not make any mistakes. There is too much money involved, and still too many loose ends. The only thing to do is we must take the car, then we can miss the airport security. It will be easier to take the guns, the IDs and the money."

Arnika paused then, smiling so her full lips curved: "And we will miss all those scam artists at the train stations, trying to help you with your ticket, or your luggage, or your seat, when all the time all they want is to pick your pocket, or take a bag, or steal some euros. I once picked the guy's pocket when he thought he was picking mine – he had more money than I had! And they also use women and children, preying on your sympathy or to distract you, while the police just look on. Why can't they try to make an honest living, like me?"

"Is there such a thing as an honest living? At least not for you," and now he was smiling.

"Seriously, we must meet with the Embassy folks who will have the route and the documents for the shipments. They will also want their cut of the proceeds...."

"As always. Their share is about thirty percent, or so they think."

"We cannot trust them."

He smiled again. "Trust no none, with nothing, nowhere, no how...."

"Even you?" It was half a question, half a barb; half that wanted to know the answer, and half that knew.

"Even me...." The answer was half a smile, half a question too.

"I need you."

"I need you too, you temptress......" The words trailed away as they kissed, softly at first, then harder and more demanding. The tongues touched and twisted, seeking the nectar of the skin and the tastes of the night.

Such sweet, liquid nectar.

A villa and a castle In Umbria

The old stone walls were laced with windows and the pink bricks of ages past. The road to the villa curled up the hill, turned past the cross and then you saw the valley of Niccone, with green trees and vines. The twisty trails all zagged and zigged up and down the hill like the snakes that lay basking in the sun.

The sounds were of silence, overlaid with breezes in the leaves and the bell chime of every hour in the old tower above the villa. It had once been a church and then a monastery, and rebuilt as a sprawling wonder of tiled floors, old wood doors with ancient sliding bolts, and rooms with shuttered windows that opened onto views over the hills and the sparkling pool. Vines clambered over the gazebo roof.

The terrace was dappled in sunshine and shade and held a few chairs and enough space on the long table for drinks, Campari and Cinzano and Chianti, sampled in round glasses and with grateful throats. The afternoon sun blazed, and lit the tangled shadows of the wisteria and grapevine twisting stems.

Swallows and swifts came and swooped and dived, aerobatic and acrobatic at the same time, dipping and swerving over the pool surface. They came together in threes and fours, as if competing for the best trick, or twisting turn. Sometimes a ripple spread from where their wings touched the water, and they turned to dive spectacularly again and again, before disappearing behind the trees.

As the evening came, so came the cool air and the pink sky as the sun went to its own bed, to lie and rest for yet another while.

In the morning, mists cloaked the valley, and the green hills, as the sun raised its lazy head again above the trees. As they awoke, the hen cackled her mournful song, and the birds sang their chirps and chirrups into the clearing blue of the sky. Arnika's eyes were open but her mind was not yet clear.

She gathered her fashionable clothes, her working gear, and her strappy shoes, showered in the tiled room, and opened the window to let the steam out and the morning in. The coffee tasted like a new wine, sharp and tangy. The mist and the mind cleared of the fog, leaving bright clear light.

Could she kill him? Should she kill him? She had loved him, yes, and hated him, and caressed him. But now, it was a choice, simple but ugly.

Would he kill her? What was the risk of letting her live, of letting him live?

Her thoughts ran as an endless stream through her mind. She would pass through this world just once- but it is the mark she would leave that matters, and the life lived. And let live.

As they drove down the narrow lanes, winding among the trees, the wild flower blooms, red poppies strewn like open hearts, and the hidden tourist houses. And then they saw the tower, high above the trees from miles away, a spike with crenelated walls, like some sentinel keeping silent watch over all that moved in the valley and the rolling hillsides.

Their car could just pass through a black metal gate that swung open as they approached, and closed immediately behind. The tower was, like everything else, an illusion, an embellishment on a massive red-tile roofed castle, rebuilt of new stones and old ideas. The shutters and bars spoke of darker times, of praying priests, armored knights and damsels always in distress.

Theatre of Words

He knew from her text messages that they were coming, and was walking slowly out to greet them as they approached the gnarled front door. His bodyguards were by his side, a burly and bearded muscle man, with a piercing gaze, and a massive dog slavering and panting. The contrast with Ivan was sharp, too thin and wispy in his body and his face. His shirt was silk, a blue tone like the sky, and his jeans a designer brand of white, with his matching Gucci sandals.

He had been the Energy Minister, a huge reward from his friend Boris for helping overthrow the old regime, until a financial scandal had brought him down. It was the usual story of yielding to temptation. The USA had been spending money, lots of money on nuclear non-proliferation to stop the key scientists leaving for nascent nuclear states who were desperate to have their own bombs. The spread of the knowledge had to be avoided. So he had helped, and had helped himself also to a little percentage of the funds.

But a little of a billion is still a lot. So when his overthrown regime was also overthrown, he would have a nest egg. The Americans were so mad at his siphoning of the money, they had tried to track him down, have him extradited to the USA, whenever he went on his travels. To access his now bulging Swiss and Cyprus bank accounts, he was lured to Zurich, and arrested in the street on a rainy, snowy day.

Once he was in police custody, both the Americans and the Russians fought over who could have his head, until he paid them back, and agreed to testify. He had used his cash to fund a drug ring and make some more cash, and the mafia took a percentage. So he was connected, but "they" were dangerous connections.

They helped to cover his tracks; they gave him this grand tower in the country, to live as a Rapunzel without the long hair.

In reality, he was an exile living in castle splendor overlooking the hills, and dreaming for his princess to come to rescue him. And here she was.

"Hello, Ivan Ivanovitch," she said. In the sun he thought she looked gorgeous, with just a hint of skin and straps and more beneath the loose and slightly transparent unbuttoned blouse, an elegant jewel on her wrist, and her hair falling in waves.

"Welcome, Svetlana, to my country abode", in perfect English, and as he kissed her his beard touched her slightly and his lips more on her cheeks. Turning to the Agent, now with more of a questioning look, "And welcome to you too, sir."

One of her many names, each one a different flavor, each an almost different life.

"May I introduce Clifford" she said, "and also may I introduce you to Ivan. By his name alone, a descendent of Ivan the Terrible, a living mogul of Italy, friend of Popes and plenipotentiaries, a man amongst men."

"Spare me, my dear, such grandeur!" but he was clearly pleased by the exaggerations.

As they shook hands, and the grips tested each other, the bodyguard had the dog sit with a single gesture and then moved just too close.

Feeling Clifford stiffen, Ivan explained, "Please raise your arms, above your head- I am sorry, but we must search you. You see, I have enemies everywhere as well as friends. Unfortunately, dressed as she is Svetlana is not searchable...much as I would like to, by myself."

The bodyguard's hands were rough and probing, as he performed the pat down and the feel. "He's clean," was all he said, in an Italian accent, and stepped back. She knew he was likely both a guardian and a watcher, perhaps protection from his unfriendly Mafioso friends.

"Follow me", and they did. Into the doorway of old wood and metal ties, with hinges and bolts as large as an arm, with the video scanner above half hidden in the archway.

Inside it was cool, and the sunbeams cast from the windows were like searchlights cutting into the shade. The flagstones led to a long vaulted hall, with chairs and shields on the stone walls, then to another door and finally a tapestried room. Here ornate scenes spoke of the armored knights of the Middle Ages, on splendid horses, fighting the battles and enemies of the past. The center of the room had a long dark wooden table and many large, heavily carved chairs.

"Sixteenth and seventeenth century, and perhaps earlier," he said, waving his arms at the walls and room. "When men were men, and woman were ...."

"It is magnificent, Ivan. As you are."

"I am glad that you like it, Svetlana. My dear, I have much, much more to show you. It is so long since we shared the good days in Moscow, and now we are here in the good days in Italy. I am glad to see you. Please sit."

They did, sinking into the cushioned chairs and being served white-foamed cappuccinos in white china, which appeared as if by magic carried by a girl, whose looks were casual chic, with a flowing red dress and olive skin. Her curves spoke of long limbs and fullness. Ivan did not introduce her, but touched her arm slightly and whispered in her ear as she bent enticingly near him to lay the coffee on the table. She left the room, catching a slight backward glance towards Clifford, while the bodyguard stood silently looking in the corner.

The dog had gone.

Another deal, another day

The table divided them, a shining expanse, but she could see he was nervous and aware that danger lurked in the room and in their conversation.

"So where have you been these last few years, Svetlana?"

She knew he was suspicious, despite the smiles and graces. "So little, you would not believe me if I told you."

"So, dear one, tell me what I would not believe!"

"In Europe, and in Moscow, translating and advising, as you know. There has been much happening- things are changing so fast. The old has gone, but the new has not emerged. I gained a nice tan on the Riviera, only to replace it with a fur coat in the winter in Moscow."

She droned on, occasionally moving her long fingers in gestures and always looking at his reactions. He did not believe her. So she exaggerated again, knowing he would know but half expected it.

"I have also just been to Firenze, the city of cities, the art of building and the art of creating, both frozen in time. The leather and the gold, the statues and the statuesque, the fashion and the fake, the clothes and the unclothed, the endless streams and crocodile files of overheated tourists. But always it is a world that is old and new at the same time, and both David and Botticelli's Venus. I bought this blouse there."

"It looks wonderful, on you," his eyes following his words.

"Thank you," She knew he had noticed the buttons and the tanned flesh, "But what have you been up to, Ivan, not your old tricks?"

His gaze was deep and penetrating. "Old ones and new ones, just like Firenze, my dear. The world has been both good to me, and bad for me. I still have influence, you know despite, the unpleasantness of the past. But now to the future. What do you want of me?"

"I need your money. I want your silence," strongly, almost as a demand. Her voice belied her hands that spread wide in a gracious, half bowing gesture.

He stiffened, ran his hands over his beard, and fired back: "Many, many people want my money. So many I cannot count. I ask what for?"

The Agent Hsu spoke, at last. He had been silently watching the charade, waiting for the others to speak, fencing with their words and smiles. Now it was time for business. Funny business.

"We are shipping some material from Africa to Europe, with the consent of the Europeans, Russians and Americans. The vessel is registered in the Bahamas, so is not subject to US inspections. The cargo will be labeled as originating in and loaded in Murmansk, the nuclear port. It must come through without interference. Your old friends in high places in Moscow who arrange and allow the shipping papers will get their cut, for their pension funds, and you cover the insurance payment."

"And what material would this be? Nothing illegal I hope", the drips of sarcasm heavy on each the word.

"Absolutely legal, of course. With all the international paperwork, even the blessing of the Pope, everything and everyone is fully protected. For you, it does not matter – the value is billions in whatever currency you count these days."

"What is my share, and my guarantee?"

"Ten percent of the proceeds, but for a guarantee in writing we need the upfront money in cash. Say, a million. Now."

He feigned surprise. "A million! How can I trust you? That is a lot of cash to have on hand and just give away, even to your best friends. Do you think that Italy has some kind of a black economy? That people do not fully pay their taxes? That suitcases exchange hands not just envelopes? That all my good friends here deal in cash? That somehow I would have such an amount at my fingertips? How could you think such a thing?"

He settled back in his chair, looking both elegant and powerful.

Arnika made her move. "You can trust me, Ivan. You will get a reward now, and a return later of many millions. As always, what I offer you is without compare", bending forward slightly as she spoke so the blouse flowed open a little lower to show the curve of her breasts. She knew even after living out of the country for so long, he still remembered, and now longed.

"Remember this." Ivan's eyes could not leave looking, and he spoke with heightened passion. "I am just acting as any banker would. But here are any problems, any late payments, and issue- any, any issue- my friends will come after you. They will find you. They will torture you. Here in the dungeon of this castle, where the tools of pain were perfected, and still exist. I can show you them if you wish – the rack to stretch your beautiful limbs and break your joints, the press to crush your fingers, and the flail to remove your tender skin, piece by piece, slowly. You will confess and regret, before they kill you. Remember this. Medieval it may be, it still works, especially on the softest flesh."

Then smiling, "I exaggerate, of course, but not too much."

"We understand."

"Good," he signaled to the bodyguard, who stepped forwards and Ivan whispered in his ear. And to his visitors, "How about we have dinner together? Tonight?"

"What a splendid idea, Ivan. I will wear my best if you take me to the best."

"My dear, for you, only the best, always."

The tension eased, at least for a while.

Dinner on the terrace

The money had indeed arrived in a white wheelie carry-on, one that was a "spinner." She had said how appropriate it was, as the money could go every and any way at the touch of a finger. Ivan had laughed, but was not truly amused.

Clifford counted it- crisp notes, neatly stacked in bundles, while Ivan and Arnika looked on, sipping an aperitif. She knew he could not resist her, and could not resist easy money. It was a toss-up as to which one he would go for first. And which one she wanted.

The evening air was warm, as the car with Ivan's driver swept her through the lanes beneath the walled city with its bustling tourist streets and stalls. Suddenly, there was life, an old building and its sign, Il Restaurante Leonardo. Not just any Lenny's bar and restaurant, but perhaps one of Leonardo da Vinci's many possible haunts where he gained inspiration and observed the world unfold as a panorama of green fields and vines below. An old estate, now a Relais, with subtle lights and roses climbing in pink profusion on metaled arches surrounding the terrace. The fountain sounded its song, tumbling from a lion's mouth.

Giant market umbrellas, arching over and giving both shade from the evening sun and a hint of informality, covered the tables. Three of the other tables were occupied. It was still early, and the couples having their trysts and celebrations whispered secretly their conversations, their lives and dreams.

She had dressed deliberately, as always with care for the occasion. The dress was black, edged with red, and cut with a swirl near the knees, and a low V in the neckline, to slightly reveal. The underwear was lacy yet loose, and her butterfly-heeled Tuscan shoes clattered slightly on the slab stones. The knife lay tight in its tiny sheath, inside her thigh.

Heads turned, as the Maitre d'Hotel in his pin-striped suit showed her to Ivan's table where he sat alone. It was laid in white cloth, with blue glasses and a candle flame flickering in its holder.

Ivan rose, greeted her again with a double kiss, and a touch on the bare arm. He wore a smart grey suit, cut to fit his slightly bulging waistline, and an open necked shirt, showing just a hint of chest. He was perspiring, slightly. Although there was no sign of the bodyguard she knew he was not far away. Courteous as always, unless angered, he greeted her, "Hello, my dear. You look radiant."

"You are still full of such flattery," she replied. "But it is nice to see you too. It has been a long time."

"Too long, my dear. How I have lived and longed for you."

"And I have longed to see you ...." and meaning it.

The meal was an assembly of courses, delicate starters, pasta first, then duck. All served with wine and plenty of toasts between them.

On the table near them, an American couple, she younger than he, started to argue about their future not being together, and how they were now totally incompatible.

As the pink sky darkened, the moon rose as a crescent, smiling sideways at them, and the stars dappled the sky. The coffee was late arriving so she skitter-scattered in her heels to the bathroom, an elegant tiled space next to an enormous wine cellar stacked with bottles in neat shelves, and with a tasting bar. Her cell phone was in her red leather bag, and so she quickly speed dialed, spoke softly, and then swaying gently flounced back to the terrace where Ivan was impatiently waiting.

She sat with a swirl of the dress, and placed her next remark carefully. "You remember my father, of course?"

The eyebrow raised slightly. "I knew him, yes." His eyes shifted away for a moment, as if seeing something.

"You know why he was attacked?" Now she was watching carefully, the wine had loosened her tongue.

"I don't know. You might say he must have crossed the wrong people. You know how it is."

She feigned ignorance, waved her hands in denial, and laughed, a laugh that echoed a little around the terrace. "No, no, no. Me?"

On the next table, the American couple were now definitely getting a divorce. Or, at least, arranging a settlement over dinner. Their voices raised and then lowered almost to a whisper. They were going to occupy separate beds, perhaps even separate rooms from now on. He wanted too much, and she wanted it all. Otherwise, it was a normal relationship. They were not angry, just seeming to be very disappointed with each other, or tired of the effort.

The wine was a local Tuscan red served in glass goblet, with tangy taste and fruity aromas of the night. The evening air was cool to her bare shoulders.

"My father knew you, I believe, quite well."

"Yes." Slowly, with a hint of a smile. "We had some dealings. You know, of the usual kind. That is why I will work with you."

"What was it, these dealings? What happened?" She could feel the wine working, warming her veins, making her relax. Must not relax too much, she thought, and be very, very careful.

"He was to deliver a package in Istanbul for some friends. Somehow there was a misunderstanding, or someone else knew of the package. They wanted it and tried to take it. I heard he somehow escaped death then, and that even some of the attackers were killed. The news was all around. Anyhow, that is history now. You must have known—he must have told you before he died?" As he sipped the coffee a hint of milk remained on his beard.

"No, he never did- he died too soon." She feigned a sob, a trace of a tear, but inside her emotions rose and sadness crept over her memories. "It is still very painful to think of it all. What was in it, this package?"

"I heard it was diamonds-so much easier to move precious stones than money, less bulky than gold. That reminds me, I have a present for you."

The small package was beautifully wrapped, and fastened with a gold bow. Small earrings, set in gold, and diamonds and emeralds glistened, catching the light.

"How lovely. How can I thank you?"

"You know how, my dear."

Yes, she knew. "Show me your tower. Now."

On the next table, aided by wine, their reconciliation was seemingly now complete. The arguing and accusations had stopped. They would live happily at least until tomorrow.

Tower of Strength

The drive was a swift descent into darkness, down the lanes, where a cat crossed on phantom feet, and the occasional screech of an owl cut the silence. The tires screeched too, on the bends, as the driver had been told to hurry. The engine roared.

They sat in the back, and she felt his hand touch her thigh, the fingers moving slowly up. He was a dark shadow. The bends meant he could not keep his touch, as they swayed with each curve. Suddenly, they were at the gates, but this time the tower and walls were lit with an amber glow, with beams that dappled and shadowed the stones and corners. It looked like a fairytale castle might look in a movie. The tower now rose almost as a shaft of light.

The driver opened the door, and Ivan took her hand, leading her through the door, the hallway and to a flight of stone stairs that spiraled ever upwards circling to the right. "Let me show you my tower."

"Not in these heels, Ivan."

"Then, we must take the elevator!" he said, and pulled back a draped curtain where a shining steel door immediately slid open. "It is a special feature- what girl would climb all those stairs anyway? Perhaps just about a hundred of them- but what girl could refuse a lift."

She could not see the bodyguard, but knew he could not be far away, perhaps tracking on video camera. There was one hidden beneath the drapery. There was another one in the elevator too, so Ivan behaved himself, just pressing buttons and humming quietly. He had drunk some vodka after dinner too, so was slightly flushed.

The elevator hummed quickly and the doors opened to the most splendid square room, with a dark beamed ceiling, subtle lights, pierced windows in semi-stone and plaster walls, and animal rugs strewn across the floor leading to a large duveted bed. There were two doors, one with a mirror, the other older one to the right, but the stairway was open as an archway. A bar and flatscreen stood on one side, together with an ornate walnut desk with a computer, a couch with great flowered cushions, and an array of books.

"My dacha, my dear, just my little cottage in the country." He was so proud. "I can tell you, my dear, that not many people live to see this room."

She scanned the room, impressed, but taking in the details, and could see no cameras or video. Suddenly, he gripped her arm, pressed his lips to hers, and held his other hand behind her back, moving it across her flesh under the dress. She could feel his tongue pressing and his beard rasping against her skin. He was slipping the shoulder of her dress down, and his breath was faster. His fingers reached for her breast, and cupped it. Arnika suddenly felt naked as he pulled at her hemline and ran his other hand up the inside of her thighs.

"Slowly, slowly, Ivan." Pulling back slightly she whispered. "We have all night."

"I do not care about the rest of the night. Only now," he was insistent, pressing, hands everywhere. He was already aroused.

"How about a drink?" trying to delay, delay, divert, divert, deflect, deflect.

"Champagne? Brandy? Amaretto? Nectar of the gods?"

"Cognac- old and strong," then half turning and gesturing, "Where does that door go?"

He was at the bar already, fumbling below for something, then opening and pouring the brandy already, quickly into the large bowls of the goblets.

"That, that is Juliet's other balcony. I will show you," passing her the part-filled glass, and moving to the door. "Look, and be amazed." He pulled back the blackened bolt and threw open the door.

She had not realized how high they were, but it was almost overpowering. The night sky was bright with stars and the crescent moon was now high in the sky, casting its own shadows. The lights of the windows of distant villas glowed, and far away a small cluster of a village. The air was clear, and still, wrapping her in the cool cloak of night. The parapet was just at waist height, but small lights showed where to tread.

She turned. He was moving right behind her, reaching for her back, his arm outstretched and thrusting. She ducked under him so fast that he missed her, merely brushing her shoulder. In his hand she thought she saw a glint, and backed against the rough stone wall.

She knew she was cut. And could feel something warm
trickle from her skin.

"Surely you did not think that I believed you, my dear.
But it is worth a million to me just to trap you, and
see you meet the same fate as your father. You have
escaped me for too long- you cost me his life, and he
cost me many millions. But you came to me, trying to
catch me – me, Ivan Ivanovitch!"

She touched the inside of her thigh, searching, and he
laughed. "And here is your knife, the one you brought
to kill me with! As if you could..." He held up the
small blade, pointing now at her throat. "And now it
is for you."

"Ivan, let me explain...."

"Explain? Explain why you and your father stole from
me? Why you came all the way to find me here? My
friends had told me you were coming. I expected
treachery, but not this, not this love charade, this
spectacularly silly show, and you to be so foolish."
His other hand started to reach towards the inside of
his coat.

It was then she moved. He had drunk too much to be
that swift, and she was still alert and fighting for her
life. He thrust the knife at her stomach, and just
missed but the blade caught in the dress folds. Razor
sharp, as she had honed it, the fabric cut away,
showing her bare skin. He wrenched at the knife as it
caught in the folds, and she could feel and hear it
tearing through the cloth, catching on the zipper at
the side for a moment and then the blade came free.

Before he could stab at her again, at that instant she
stepped sideways, took hold of his other arm, and

twisted it behind him, turning him towards the parapet as she stepped away from the wall.

He stumbled forward a little, letting go of the knife but now reaching inside his coat with his free hand. She yanked his arm higher up his back, and struck him quickly on the neck with the edge of her hand. It hurt her but also stunned him. He grunted and dropped the little black gun from his hand, and it clattered on the stones......

He called out. "Help!! Quickly!!" as she forced his body half over the parapet, twisting his arm up even further. He called out again, but this time in pain. "Aaaah....aaaaah.... stop...stop.... you are breaking my arm...."

"Look down, Ivan, and enjoy the view," as she simply pinned him against the parapet. He was now trying feverishly to get free, and swinging his free arm back, but his breath was now coming in pants and puffs.

"Niet, niet, no more, please. Let's say we are even," he gasped, "Just back off, let me go, and I will give you even more money. More than you could ever want. I want to enjoy the rest of my life and you can enjoy yours."

"You still can," she said, "but it is just very short."

Her other arm was now pressing on the back of his neck, bending his head further forward while she twisted his arm even higher behind his back, bending his whole body as well further over the parapet.

"Who are you working for?"

"Not you any more, not ever," and pushed him.

He was unbalanced and heavy, and tried to strike her with his elbow and to free his locked arm. Then he was gone, falling, falling into the light and shade of the walls. His fall ended in a dull thump, and with a quick look she could just see his body spread-eagled on the courtyard below, face up, staring, arms moving slightly.

Then she heard the elevator: he must have summoned the guard when seeming to fumble at the bar. Arnika picked up the gun, a 9mm semi-automatic with the safety catch off, and scooped up her knife now streaked with her own blood. She ran across to the stairway, and could hear a dog's claws on the stone steps, running, panting and growling. Now which way?

The Way Out

There were the stairs and the dog, the elevator and the guard, or the balcony and the fall.

She quickly checked herself, and her self-control. Lucky, the cut was superficial as was the slit in her dress. Again she checked the safety catch was off on the gun, and there was a round in the chamber. She crouched behind the bed, as the elevator arrived just before the dog.

The doors slid open, and he darted out of the elevator, crouching, so her first shot missed, but the second caught him just above the knee. He half crumpled to one side, and then she could not see him from behind the bed where she had squatted for cover, and for surprise. The sounds deafened her and him, reverberating around in this tower room, while the bullets ricocheted off the stones with a high "tang" sound.

He fired back, a short burst of semi-automatic rounds, which with a muzzle silencer sounded like a chattering rhythm. Arnika rolled under the bed, and saw him just aiming his black AR15 towards her, his face grimaced in pain, but his eyes glassy cool. Her first shot hit him in the neck, blood spurting and squirting, and the second in the body. His shots all went high as he fell backwards, causing flints of stone to burst from the wall. He collapsed, a lifeless heap.

The room smelt of the acrid smoke, and filled with a blue haze.

The dog now stood panting at the top of the stairway, tongue and teeth showing, waiting for the command that did not come. So well trained, so obedient.

There was no more time to pause or wait. She wiped the fingerprints off the handle of the gun with the hem of her dress. Holding it by the edge of the hammer, she tossed it over the parapet to clatter next to Ivan's still moving body.

Off with her heeled shoes, and then past the dog, down the uneven steps lit by LED lights at the sides. The courtyard was empty, so quickly now she was running towards the gate. She heard a groaning in the dark nearby, and there was Ivan, sprawled out, still staring skywards towards that golden moon, and his tower. Arnika could not stop to say goodbye, but squeezed through the gap by the side of the gate and out into the road.

The car was sitting in the shadows just where they had agreed. She flung open the door, and the engine turned into life.

"Thank you...Thank you," Arnika was almost breathless.

"Did it go OK?"

"Yes, just as we planned, but a little tougher than I thought. I am cut but OK."

"Let's go. Vamanos!"

They sped away into the darkness, into the night. The headlights led the way, into safety.

Chapter 3

Echoes of the Future

Echoes of the future

As the car sped away, she dabbed at the blood. The sight made the memories came flooding came back, her mind racing...

When she was young, a teenager, she thought her legs were too fat, her skin too pale, and her breasts too small. The mirror then showed a gangly girl, with eyes that looked back as deep pools and irises of multi-hues.

Her father's Russian accent tinged her voice; her mother's French accent tinged her fashion sense. They had met in the last great Terrorist Wars that had racked Africa, the East, the Urals, and the contested Gulf; when the religious extremists of every color had combined to fight, overthrow the dictators, old family regimes and economic colonials.

And almost won, but for the intervention of Russia, the USA and Europe, with their drones, strafing planes, robotic missiles and money. It almost bankrupted them, while China, Iran, India, Brazil and many others looked on and applauded their folly and loss of life. But, as always, money was to be made as well as lost.

She had been a translator, euro languages to anything, and He had been a soldier, an officer and a treaty negotiator. Which was how they met, one hot steaming day, in Mali or somewhere, with swaying breezes, a long table, piles of papers, diplomatic armored vehicles, and blue-helmeted guards for the diplomats and translators. All gathered so the politicians could agree how to carve up the oil, gas and uranium for the next twenty years or until the next failed revolution, failed dictator, or failed UN resolution occurred.

And He and She agreed to form their own alliance, their own union, their own partnership, bound by a treaty of love.

Arnika had been born soon after, an orphan of the e-age, where relationships, friends and education were all downloaded, along with recipes, books and orders for guns. They had moved incessantly from here to there, the jungles of Africa, the city deserts of Europe, across the plains of Ukraine.

This was the age of selective diplomacy, where some were to have missiles, and some not, some allowed nukes, some not, and some regimes were to change. Thus, she gathered knowledge, of politics, money and death, as the struggle to carve out the new world order from the old world disaster continued unchecked under the guise of the growing and greedy global economy. Everyone depended on who they knew, who they could know, and what they knew.

Her parents made mountains of money in side deals, bought condos in the cities, villas in the countries, and time-shares in the warmth. They lived life.

Meanwhile, while they helped destroy and remake the world, Arnika went to good international schools, was an excellent runner, and a balanced athlete, who enjoyed the one-on-one sports and competing head-to-head. She loved languages, history and art, but her favorite was literature, where she gorged on the great novels, Anna Karenina, Madam Bovary, and spy thrillers like Ian Fleming, and of course Smiley's People.

Her classmates and her non-friends called her "Arny," but not because of her aptitude for golf. The size of her wardrobe matched her bank balance before she graduated, and went to work on her own deals, first helping her father. He taught her how to handle the automatics and the semi-automatics: where to aim to kill, to play cards and aim to win, and how to confront and when to retreat. And how to make a deal.

Her mother taught her how to handle the boys and the men: where to aim to thrill, to play the field and aim to win, how to approach and how to disengage. The life skills came quickly, as did the lovers and the losers.

It was fun. Until that fateful day in Istanbul, that still seemed like just yesterday.

The beginning of the end

Then, the shadows of the day draped the ancient Constantinople city walls in golden colors. The minarets and market stall made a patchwork of noise, smells and people buying herbs, spices and lachoum. Everywhere, the bridges ran with traffic, the waterways with ferries, the streets with honking cars, and the Sophia with tourists straining their necks and wallets.

She had flown in from Moscow, on an early flight leaving at 4 in the morning, when the sleeping city had not disgorged its traffic, and the snow had let the flights leave. The security scanning was waived, given her Orlov credentials and contacts, and her luggage had bedazzled the porter as much as the tip.

The taxi stopped outside the main steps. The hospital room had empty walls, a few chairs, and many blinking lights and humming machines. He lay still on the rumpled bed, with tubes and pipes, cables and wires draped almost everywhere. A drip slowly dripped into the clear tube that ran into his bandaged and labeled wrist. The floor gleamed; the bandages and masks lay discarded on the sheets. His breath was shallow, the color of the face slightly grey, the smile a little forced, the lines on the face and around the eyes deep with pain.

"How are you, Father?" she said as she circled the room, then took his hand briefly. It was cool but clasped her fingers.

"Shot three times," his voice weak and breath hard. "It could be worse." He coughed slightly, and she could feel him trembling. "The morphine works for a while."

"How? Why? Who?" The questions tumbled out in no special order.

"I should have known...." his breathing a little harder, his voice softer. "They were waiting for me, just outside the gates to the compound. I think there were four of them, with semi-autos. Lucky I had my vest on, otherwise I would be raw meat just shot to pieces. I rolled out of the car, firing my 9mm. They ...."

"Slowly, slowly, take it easy. Love you...."

"...they kept up a good fire, but I know I got one in the leg. In return they got both of mine," motioning to the blankets and the tubing. "One is pretty bad."

"Can you walk?"

"Walk _! I will be lucky if I can crawl the rest of my life." He paused to look at her. "Broke the bone in one for sure. Anyway, they took off when the guards came out, but it was too late. Jan was with me- he took the first rounds full on and is very dead."

"Jan?"

"My partner in crime."

"So now you have no guard. Where is Mother?" She knew the answer.

"At what she does best- a fashion show in Paris, I bet. If she was here in Istanbul, she would be dead by now. We are all in danger...", and for the first time fear showed in his words and in his eyes.

"Why?"

"You know our work, our dealings.... well we have crossed a someone who is too big and just too dangerous this time."

"Who?"

He motioned to her to bend over nearer, raising a finger to his dry lips, and she let her breasts brush his shoulder, and her breath brush his cheek.

He whispered in her ear, a voice now drowned from those listening by the machines pulsing and ticking.

It was then she heard the door move behind her, a slight movement, and her father stiffened and his eyes widened.

She released his hand, and dropped to one knee, slightly behind the bed rail, her hand now already reaching for and touching the grip of the gun in her shoulder bag.

The end of pain

"Time for the meds and for those vital life signs," the grey shape said, carrying a tray and wheeling a grey cart with drawers and handles. "How are we today? And who are you, my pretty lady?"

Arnika was already wary, but slowly raised herself, not releasing the pistol grip. "His daughter. And who are you?"

"Today, I am his best friend ..." with a slight smile, "I bring the end of all pain," motioning at the tray with a row of bottles, small cups and plastic packages, and a needle, and the cart with its set of drawers.

She saw the grey shape look over at the blood pressure monitor, and its blinking pulsing heart rate.

Moving around the bed, with its array of charts and screens, it was then Arnika saw the shoes. Now shoes can tell you a lot about somebody, more than the clothes sometimes, of wealth, status, job, last known walk, the country of origin, the height of the girl, the weight of the man. For Arnika they were part of her fashion sense, and her sixth sense. She remembered the smart set, the running set, the health nuts, the high heels and the low life shoes. These did not seem right- they were dirty, just a little aged, and had scuff and scratch marks as if from being dragged along the ground, on their side.

There was a speck of dark on one side, and suddenly she knew she was staring, why she was staring, and who she was staring at from just two feet away.

The grey shape saw it too, and moved first, reaching for the pocket of the loose coat with the spare right hand. The pistol came out of Arnika's bag, just as the pistol came out of the pocket. But she kicked him first, in a place you do not want to kick with her hard and pointy toes. The extreme MMA training had paid off again, as it had on that date night when the gallant and elegant dinner guest unexpectedly became a late-night wannabe sex fiend.

The low grunt, and doubling up happened together, so she kicked again, aiming now at the lowered face, catching him right on the nose. Something crunched, and blood drops sprayed the floor as he crumpled and then fell backwards, sending the cart and the tray flying. The gun skitter-scattered across the floor as he let it fall. He tried to get up, groaned, collapsed, and tried again.

Arnika looked at her father —and he looked at her. He mouthed the words "Go...go now... go now."

She looked at the doorway, and the empty hallway, and the half-open window. There was nowhere to go. The little 38 caliber six-shot pistol was still in her hand, so she handed it quietly to her father, who slid it under the covers.

She picked up the other gun- a 9mm with a silencer, fully loaded, chromed and new.

As the grey shape tried to rise, struggling to breathe, she hit him again in the now bloodied face, but this time with the barrel of the pistol across the temple and the eyes, and he collapsed again, with more blood now from the temple, holding his battered hands to his head. With her heel she penetrated the neck, and drove the spike in as far as it would go. Then out. A quick look at the pockets, and there was another loaded magazine.

She un-hooked the BP monitor, the cardio monitor, the drip line and the EKG cable. "We will wait for them down the hallway, where they do not expect us to be. If you feel too much pain, it is not my fault. You got into this mess, now I must get us out of it."

The bed wheeled easily enough once the brake was off, and the last tangle of power cables undone. Father groaned most of the way, gentle groans of both pain and pride. The hall was deserted, just mirrors and signs but no people, no cleaners, no staff, no guards. They must have all been paid or warned to not be present. It was just like in the Godfather movie, she thought.

Down the hall was a small alcove, leading to a teaching room, or so said the sign. With a deep sigh she stopped, and pushed the door open, slid the bed inside.

"Stay here."

"Can't do anything else' he gasped, "Just. Point me over to the side, where I can get a clear shot if needed. Good luck, my girl."

A kiss blown, a wave of the hand and then she stepped back out, onto to the polished tiles and plastic. The 9mm and her wits were all she had.

Blood on her hands

Pressed against the wall, she could hear them coming, steps of perhaps three, hurrying. The voices urgent, accented.

"He should have called by now, or come out. The dead should be dead by now."

"The room is down here to the right. The number is 101, intensive care or something like that. Ivan said it would be empty here, but for him."

Who is Ivan?
How did they know the room?
Who paid off everyone?
Can I kill them?

"No sweat, my dear, we can finish it off anyway-...I'll call in now to report."

"What the hell! Look at this! He's gone.... but Amal is here, looks like he never made the assignment. He's all busted up."

"Let's take Amal and skip, there'll be another time."

"We cannot go back empty. He will kill us if we don't kill him."

"Where the hell is he? We only have five more minutes, then the guards will come back."

Voices, more voices. She had never held her breath for so long, nor wanted to pee so much. Her mind was focused on the moment, the need to suddenly spring the rehearsed move, dropping forward to one knee, lifting the gun to eye level, firing the three, four, five shots, aiming first for the bodies, and then for the kill. She stayed poised to strike.

"He was supposed to be immobile," said a voice. "That's what the e-profile and info said. Cannot move, bedridden. We should have finished it at the compound yesterday... now..."

"It's dialing.

Hello, hello.

Hi, chief, looks like he skipped or had help. Amal's beaten up, but there's no one here.

OK. OK, yes, I know we screwed up.

 OK, a second screw up.

I know we should have known. But the chip did not pick up his move, and the place is empty. Yes, empty.

Yes. No one.

OK. OK."

"What did he say?"

"He said to skip now, come back to the task when he is discharged. We can work it then using the cyber chip. Let's go."

"What about Amal?"

"No problem – he fouled up. Hey, Amal, look at me, no just a little to the left...Sorry, Amal." There were two quick shots from a silencer. "Let's go."

The footsteps and voices faded down the hallway- she let her breath exhale. The gun now felt heavy, the palms of the hands moist, the ankle and her leg ached from the kicks. Turning back through the doors, back towards the bed, he was lying at an odd angle, his face averted. So she reached forward and tried to straighten him. She felt something wet, and pulled back.

There was blood on her hands.

As the car sped away, with a tissue she dabbed off the blood of her own family.

Chapter 4

Formal Inspection

The Good Guys

Chief Inspector Luigi Farini struggled out of bed, woken around three in the morning by the cell phone buzzing near his head. The message was urgent, and short. He showered fast, grabbed his always packed and ready overnight bag, and checking his gun belt, clattered down the marbled steps of the apartment onto the empty Via Strazzi where the car was waiting.

He had already a busy schedule with a lot of travel, so waking early was just like being on another international assignment. Time shifts and jet lag really meant nothing to him now: he slept on planes as soon as they took off, or anywhere he could rest his head. He was an awful travel companion, and now he dozed in the back seat of the speeding car.

The drive in the early hours had started on the Autostrada from Roma, but then, as soon as they turned off in Umbria had been full of dark curves and hedges. Here, the blaring sirens and flashing lights of the police car were his only protection against a cow in the road, or a slightly inebriated tourist or some local resident navigating the narrow back roads after dinner. He had not liked being woken up, and even less coming to this place.

When they arrived at the Tower, looming like a spike against the early morning sky, the space beyond the gates was full of police cars, more lights, an ambulance with its doors open and a stretcher halfway out, and milling policemen. He waved his credentials and they waved him through.

Farini got out of the car, surveyed the carnage and sighed. He was tall, elegant in a slightly untidy way, handsome in an Italian way, with a slight day's beard growth already, and a fashionable scarf knotted around his neck. His linen jacket was now thrown halfway over his shoulders, and the gun at his waist glinted briefly in the beams of the headlights.

"Ciao, Luigi, good to see you. I asked for you as soon as I knew what had happened." A slightly sweating palm gripping his hand, and the smell of coffee and garlic wafting in the air. It was his old carabinieri colleague, Francisco, greeting him, sweating slightly and looking very harassed.

"That's only because you don't want to take the blame for this one, or the heat," Luigi pulled him aside. "What happened?"

"We don't know."

"You don't know? Don't try that one on me. Of course you know."

"Ok, he's nearly dead. He isn't able to talk, at least for now. That we know. He fell- that we know- and really he should be dead."

"How did it happen?"

"Well, it was not a game they were playing at the top, not in his torre magnifico."He gestured up the stone column of the tower. "There was gunplay up there: there is a dead guard up there too. You should know that he was one of ours."

"What?" Luigi felt he was not being told everything, and said so, irritated by the lights from the cars and the whole scene of confusion. Plus there were signs of the nosey paparazzi already outside the gateway with their cell phones and cameras. "Ok, tell me everything. But show me everything first."

Francisco took him on a tour of the tower, from bottom to top, up the elevator and down the stairs. In the elevator he spoke quickly.

"Option one- he was pushed off the tower, or option two, he fought with his own guard. There are bullet holes everywhere. The dog saw it all, but he's not talking."

"You said the guard was one of ours?"

"Yes, it was Giuseppe, one of our own heavies. No one should know about this, but I am sure it will get out. Your people knew about him."

He waved towards the ambulance. "He is, or was Ivan Ivanovitch, very well connected with the Russian oligarchs, the Russian and Italian Mafiosa, and, God forbid, the Vatican. He was a real big shot once. He knew how the money moved from Russia, and around Europe from Italy. And he knew who moved it, what soccer teams were bought and what games were fixed, and where the drugs went. He knew it all, likely just knew too much."

Francisco was really upset, waving his arms and gesturing. "He knew who was targeted and who killed who. You know the story of the big wheel Russian connections in Italy, and that government committee investigation where everyone was frightened of being decapitated or poisoned. We were protecting him, and he was due to testify against them. He had lots of money, so in return for some small favors like not being put in jail, and his life being protected, we promised him a safe haven wherever he chose to live. But now...who knows..." his voice trailing off in frustration.

"Who else knew he was here?"

Francisco calmed down a little. "Well, this is a small community. Everyone knows everyone, you know how it is, Luigi." Luigi nodded and smiled. "And when a stranger with money to spend, a Russian accent, and a bodyguard moves into the village, and casually renovates a small fortress, people get to ask questions. And, of course, people soon get to know the answers, at the supermercado, the bank, the hairdressers, the bar, the restaurants. And he was not shy with the local girls. We think he had dinner, making overtures to some nice piece of fashionista, but we don't know yet which one."

Francisco paused. "So the word of where he was, it was always going to get out. Our friends in the money business would soon know his hiding place. In today's chitter chatter e-world, and instant messaging there is nothing we can do to stop that info spreading. We could see signs of messaging about him in our internet tracking system, but did not connect all the dots to think this might happen so soon."

Farini had the picture, and knew more than he was saying he knew. "Seems he would have been safer in Russia. Or anywhere else without easy extradition laws. Could be it might even be the Russians or their friends who got to him first, but they would have poisoned him, given him a big radiation dose in his wine or pasta sauce. So perhaps it is one of the Families: it's more their style to push him off a tower. Will he live?"

"Who knows…? Even if he survives this, he won't survive for long afterwards. The special prosecutor only wanted him to live long enough to testify." Francisco waved his hand at the white ambulance now pulling away, flashing its lights, with a police car following. "We have lost a witness, torched a lot of money and blown a lot of time." He shrugged, "Perhaps, maybe he will still live. Oh, and one other thing."

"Yes, what other thing?"

"We are through- nothing left for us to protect now, except the hospital bed, and perhaps his corpse. It's now up to you, the good guys to track the bad guys. You must find out who did this, and why. I understand your Minister's office has already OK'd you for this task, but do double check. And do keep your eyes open – you never know it might be it's a girl."

Farini feigned surprise. "Why do you say that?"

"There's been some e-traffic, some word out on the streets, that there is a hit-girl out there. Works for hire most likely. We have tried tracking her, but she can shape-shift too easily, and moves on quickly. But if she exists she seems very well connected and only works big time stuff. This hit would fit her mode and type of work."

Farini was already on his phone, calling his contacts, sending out feelers and warnings.

Rogue's Gallery

The morning light cast shadows across the open vista of the Piazza Signorella. The magnificent statues of David, Theseus, and their mythic huge friends, stood in frozen pose under the loggia outside the Palazzio Vecchia, with its grand façade and Florentine tower.

The tourists stood in lines like ants by the entry and ticket gates of the Uffizi Courtyard, with its columned sides, with scaffolding that spider-webbed around the new building. Cameras and cell phones clicked their pictures to fill the albums and hard drives of the multitudes of the crowds.

These frozen moments and images would live forever, as the statues had already done for hundreds of years. The greatest works of art in the world were gathered in this building, this Gallery of galleries, whose courtyard led to the arches of the Ponte Vecchio bridge.

Huddled on this ancient bridge, straddling the Arno River, were the houses and shops where goldsmiths still displayed the treasures, rings, bracelets and jewels to adorn the skin of the rich and fabulous. Their windows shone with golden glow and sparkling reflections, the price tags discretely turned over and away, so as to not deter the curious but to entice the fatal question, "How much?"

Luigi Farini strolled past the lines over to the side entrance of the Gallery, in the shade of the morning sun, and was greeted at the barrier by a uniformed guard. The entry was through a glass door, and then a scanner, all designed to stop ordinary people coming in and extraordinary art objects going out. He showed his badge and his gun, and was waved him through. The reception desk did not know where the meeting was to be held: he just asked the way to Room B662.

He climbed effortlessly up the marbled stairs, set away from the public entrance that was crowded and crushed. The majestic and plastered ceilings rose above the grand statues in their niches on the walls, their gestures and faces frozen forever. He was in the administration building, but just close to the galleries, with their frescoes, Michelangelos, Titians, Rembrandts, and sex and violence clad as art. He paused briefly to look at the second-rate art on his way to the meeting room. As often happened, the air conditioning was not working well that day. Perhaps there had been a power interruption again. The air was still and oppressive to him, even though the windows were open and the heavy brocade drapes stirred slightly in the breeze.

He saw the motion detectors and CCTV tracking him as he made his way to Room B662, which was off a long corridor lined with drapes drifting in the breeze, and endless marble, bronze and chiseled busts of Caesars and Popes.

He even thought he recognized some of them, and recalled that the Romans were masters of economy as well as war, by just having interchangeable heads for the multitude of statues that announced the Empire and stood guard throughout the known world. So when one Caesar overthrew another, or one Pope succeeded his pious predecessor, all they had to do was to ship out a new load of heads, to replace the old ones on the unchanged bodies. And the old ones ended up in storage piles, and eventually in museums, if they had not been totally ransacked, vandalized or used as building ornaments.

The sign on the door said B662 in faded gold lettering, and was also marked "Divieto di Accesso," which he ignored and without knocking turned the old brass handle. It was not really a meeting room, more a sitting area surrounded by art and antiques. Three people sat in this splendor, waiting.

A Religious Connection

Their chairs were rich in carvings and laden in red cushions. The man in a rumpled linen suit rose first, advanced directly towards Farini, his face somber, his arm outstretched to shake his hand.

"Thank you for coming, Farini. We have not met before—I am Carlo Mostetti, from the gallery, who I represent." He waved his arms around the walls. "Forgive these humble surroundings- I did not want to use my office, as this would let others know something was happening. We," and he gestured now towards the other two seated figures, "we all need your help."

The robed Bishop rose to greet him. "My dear Inspector Farini, we meet again. Or should I say Chief Inspector..."

Farini kissed the proffered and limp hand of Bishop Carlotti as a good catholic should, noting the raised veins and the ornate gold ring. "May I introduce Senior Assistant Secretary Monsignor Brandosa, from the Instituto pro Bona Publica Religiosa."

The other man rose. He was chubby, perhaps almost overweight, but extremely well dressed. He exuded both charm and malice at the same time, but his Italian accent seemed like it was from New York, mostly Brooklyn with a little Bronx and Manhattan thrown in.

"Farini, eh? Good to meet you, or should I say, not so pleased?"

Mostetti defused the conversation and the confrontation, saying, "Let's sit and enjoy the cappuccino," and as they settled and drank their fine foam from the blue Murano glasses he continued.

"Farini, we have a problem. Now everyone has problems, some big and some small." With a shrug and a wave of his hands, continuing, "Here in Florence we have been plagued by scandals: scandals at the council, of "bunga bunga" parties, of payoffs, bribery, and illicit sex. Even the Cardinal has called Florence a den of iniquity."

He continued, now more agitated and leaning towards Farini.

"Well, the money to fund these things, and to ensure silence, and to finance pensions as well as these parties has to come from somewhere. As you well know, it is most likely from a bank or from crime, or both. You remember the collapse of the Banco Ambrosiono some years ago, and the scandals because the Vatican owned it and appeared implicated, not to mention the usual signs of money laundering. And some people paid not with cash but with their lives as well."

Farini nodded, remembering the banker's body hanging beneath the bridge, as Mostetti paused briefly then quickly added: "That was bad enough. But of course, these things and the greed do not go away, as the financial crises in Europe and on Wall Street show so well."

"A deep breath almost a sigh. So now we have yet another situation with even more international implications. There are signs of money being transferred where we not have the proper controls, even after the outside audits and the reviews and the special prosecutor report. Some of it is probably in virtual money or cyber funds, something called QuidCoins™ or the like, where there are no receipts and no paper trail. Many unsavory things have been found out and disclosed already and some have been punished for these crimes and lapses. But there seems to be more happening in this new instant electronic age, with its virtual currencies and swapping and trading of derivatives and insurance bonds..."

His paused, just briefly, then, "Naturally, here in Italy, it may involve criminal elements. But we cannot be sure, or even talk openly about this. People can lose their jobs and even their lives over such matters. That is a real hazard." Then turning to the Bishop, "Monsignor, explain, please."

The Bishop was used to making explanations. Of harassment suits, of papal decrees, of new edicts, and had an impressive manner, and a great sense of occasion. His words were directed at Farini, but could have been directed at a congregation, or an assembly of Bishops, or even to a lecture hall filled with devotees or pious pilgrims.

The religious collection

The pictures on the walls, of angels and saints, and flying cherubs in their ornate golden frames, had seen it all before. He started slowly, laying out his thesis.

"What I now tell you is very sensitive. It is Monsignor Brandosa's house of good work, the Institute for Religious Public Good that we call the IPBR, which has and is the problem. It is not a bank as such, but an investment house, a needed merchant that oversees and takes care of much of our funds, and those of all the religious Orders for the nuns and priests. And also for all the musei, the many charities, the donations, the bequests, and for the expenses of the Vatican itself. We have a lot of expenses. The IPBR has many, many billions in assets, a giant cash flow, and free access to accounts and other deposits all around the religious world, also with other banks and merchant bankers."

None of the angels seemed surprised by this unfolding revelation, but Farini could see the Bishop

Carlotti was disturbed and anxious, fiddling with his Bishop's ring as he continued.

"But what is new and happening now, today, is that money and these QuidCoins™ are being traded and moved in stocks, bonds and debts, and it is really IPBR's money and its holy reputation that is being used as collateral. It is literally sucked into handling these energy stocks, energy market futures, oil corporation bonds and tradable emissions credits. This is because energy is a truly international commodity, and there are huge differences in prices and demand between Europe, India, China Russia the US and elsewhere, and IPBR exists in all these places.

"So vast sums are being shifted around, and the asset value, or the energy price, and the commodity futures value varies day-by-day, from country to country. Just think about how many millions of litres of fuel oil, or gallons of gasoline, or shale gas are literally burnt or go up in smoke each and every day."

His voice was now indignant.

"Now we are a world-wide religious order, a revered church, and a Holy City, not stock market manipulators, virtual currency manipulators and energy traders. But such work in His Name does turn in a nice reward or return on our blessed investments.

"So, occasionally, just occasionally, we- or really IPBR- indeed partake in this worldly gift from God to increase the return for helping our Public Good activities. More poverty relief, enhanced missions, added help for the needy."

His voice turned steely, and louder, becoming almost commanding.

"But something has been and is being skimmed off the top. As each transaction is made, the in and out value matches, but somehow do not match with our accounting books. It is just like the London Whale trader case, where no-one knew who is betting on what, and when, what the real value is, and how much is really being made or lost. But we know from the trading data that the largest problems is centered in the accounts here in Firenze and in Roma."

While the splendid Renaissance images looked down silently, Farini could not hold back any longer, the whole story was so fantastic yet so likely. "Sounds like a matter for the international bankers, and their Basel Rules and for your Institute management, not for me."

However, he was intrigued, so asked. "And what does all this have to do with the Gallery?"

The Gallery connection

On this cue, Mostetti now took his turn, motioning with his hands, also clearly worried and anxious. It was time for open confession, and contrition "Well, that is the other part of our story...and unfortunately our problem. We may ask God for forgiveness, but unfortunately we also need your help."

Farini could see that Brandosa's face now looked slightly sweaty, as the room heated from the morning sun that streamed through the windows. The gallery paintings now cast their own shadows, and all the past tragedies and glories of the saints hung on their words. The sins of the present were not yet fully revealed.

"The confession is that it is our account in Brandosa's Institute, in IPBR, that is the one that is being used to move this money around. You see we also have an open and large account at the Institute- that covers the loan programs, our insurance, our travelling exhibits, our cash from the public admittance at Galleries like this one, and the government grants, rebuilding, and of course, the acquisitions of property and the sales of fine art."

He held his hands as if holding a precious object.

"Art is a very tradable commodity too, and very collectible- it does not go up in smoke and its value and scarcity increase. One painting by an old master or even by a modernist can be worth ten to a hundred million these days. We have cooperation agreements and mutual transfers for shows and exhibits with all the great museums and galleries in the world- the Tretyakov in Moscow, the Louvre in Paris, the Metropolitan in New York, the Prado in Spain, the Getty in California, and so on and so on. Plus of course the private collections in the stately homes, villas, casinos and palaces in US, Europe and the UK. It is a list of who is who in the art world, and they are all connected via the auction houses too."

The pictures on the walls all knew how their lives had changed over the years, from being simply religious artifacts to works of immense significance and value.

"Now connect that web of assets to the oil and gas business trading floors, and to the major energy players, the international oil companies and corporations, plus the Middle East sheiks and the Russian oligarchs, who also collect art and valuable properties at outrageous prices. The size and scale is beyond belief. So is the opportunity for someone to take a cut of the action, whatever and whenever something is bought or sold.

Even the FBI and the US money tracking systems have no idea about this, because these are not open transactions, but shielded and hidden ones."

In the modern world, the black gold of oil also paid for the cartoons of Michelangelo and da Vinci's Renaissance, as well as for Warhol and Banksy's cartoons. Carlotti stirred, breathed heavily, and interrupted with a dismissive wave of his hand.

"It is therefore a very, very sensitive matter..."

Pausing briefly he then continued. "As you know, our new Pope is very concerned about the ethical appearance of the Mother Church, the fact that the church and its servants should be seen to be more humble and act more in God's name for the poor and for the needy. The Holy See cannot have another public scandal, not now, after all that has happened already.So the Holy Father wants to shut down the worst of the accounts and clean up the messy management of the Institute's business."

The Russian connection

Brandosa now clearly felt the pressure, speaking quickly and in a low tone. "Now perhaps I should not say this. But any religion is really like a business: it competes with others, it must fund outreach and pilgrimages, make investments and repairs in buildings, pay for its workers, and still pay its way. So, it must keep solvent and keep their shareholders and investors happy, who in this case are the flock. So it is not our fault that to execute all the divine needs we must have money. But there is a major issue."

He paused, carefully choosing his words, and Farini felt his senses prickle, waiting for the real confession.

"The Holy Father does not and could not know. No one can tell him that much of the money for those beloved, worthy and key funded programs for the poor and the needy, and indeed for the running the entire business, largely comes from highly suspect trading of energy profits, emissions credits and from dealings in art using his and God's very own merchant bank!"

Farini was pleased to see Brandosa sweat and squirm a little, so intervened. "I have the picture and I see the problem. But what exactly is it you want me to do?"

Brandosa was not schooled in smooth communication. "Surely, Farini, you know that Ivanovitch was the key man in making and moving the money? Until of course he was found skimming off the top by his employers. And now that he has been, let us say, incapacitated by persons or persons unknown, we have found that the account has been plundered. He or someone he knew took a lot of the money very recently, right from under your nose and ours!"

Mostetti swept to his feet and gestured towards another door, neatly hidden by the paneling on the side of the room.

"As you can tell, I repeat this is very high level, very sensitive, and very urgent. Now if you two gentlemen would excuse us for a moment, Farini and I must have some important words alone to discuss that very matter further. We will return in few minutes."

"Please follow me," gesturing towards the door.

An offer

Farini followed. It was an even darker, paneled room, with a small desk, a decorative alabaster lamp and a green velvet couch. And by the small window two figures were intertwined in passionate and full embrace, enjoying a sensuous kiss, the folds of their skimpy outfits outlining the many curves and clinging to the mounds of their bodies.

He saw Farini look at the marble sculpture, and spoke softly. "An unknown masterwork by a true master. It used to be called profane art, and was banned. So was formed the secret collections of the Gallery, and in the musei here and elsewhere, where there was much that was openly pornographic, and much art that was deemed just too risqué for public viewing. This one, as you can clearly see, is anatomically perfect, while its acceptable public version has been – how can I say this- suitably altered. So the original has been hidden from the public for centuries, where only the most decadent and wealthy could, let us say, enjoy and admire it. Today, with the internet, and society's new values, this decadence is everywhere."

He sighed. "There is no such thing as being unacceptable any more, only being, let us say, inappropriate or just too explicit."

"It reminds me of someone...somewhere," said Farini, gazing at this masterpiece of sacred erotica.

"It reminds everyone of someone! Or at least, of someone in their dreams!"

"What is it you want?"

He moved closer to Farini and to the statue, its rounded breasts almost touching his face. "We know you are on the Ivanovitch case so you have the inside information. Who he dealt with, where it happened and how much was involved.”

As Farini arched his eyebrows in a quizzical look, Mostetti continued. “Do not be too surprised, like you our sources are everywhere too. It is very simple: we just want our money back. No more, no less. We want this to be done quietly and quickly, before the Institute’s accounts are re-examined in a few months time. We want you to find it for us.”

He saw Farini stiffen, so paused and spoke with a soft confidence.

“Whatever, you find and whatever monies are returned, you will be well rewarded. Find out who did this, and stop them. We do not care what measures it takes. We will cover all your expenses and provide a very large retainer. In cash. You can hire who you want and pay for them. Why, we can even give you this statue that you gaze at so much!! This reward will not just be in Heaven: it will be many, many times your Inspector salary, and will multiply your pension funds by at least ten times. You may resign from the international crime force unit, or stay as you wish: we do not care. What you decide, it is up to you. We also want not just complete confidentiality and absolute discretion, but require your complete silence. No one can know who you are working for,” and waving towards the statue and the door, “this conversation and this meeting did not even ever occur.”

Farini was not sure as whether to show indignation, surprise or pleasure. He was being offered a lot, but in return his reputation and his job were on the line.

“And if I do not wish to do this?”

"You would be well advised to accept this very modest request. Not only will it make you rich, your future is assured. I am also sure there will be other occasions where a man of your skills and knowledge will be needed."

"When do you need an answer?"

"Well now, of course, before you leave."

Decisions

They had returned briefly to the main room and exchanged a few pleasantries before taking their leave of each other.

Luigi almost skipped down the marble stars, and out into the now bright sun. He felt both outwardly alert and inwardly thoughtful at the same time. The crowds of tourists had increased, and there was a hum and chatter of many different languages from the lines now stretching outside the roped off "Entrada" and "Biglietti" signs. The cameras and crowds collided in confusion and ordered chaos.

No cars were allowed in this crowded quarter of the old city, and it was easier to walk. On his way to the railway stazione he hurried through the piazza, on past the masterpiece of the Duomo, with its huge blocks of amazing black and white stones gleaming in the sun, and capped by its majestic and ancient dome.

He could not help but think of the bishop, and the difference between the façade and the reality.

These were all a scenic and unseen background to the smart set, of celebrities, actors and politicians, plus the wannabees and the inherited wealth, trading their money and influence, buying their way into the social whirl that easy money yields, of jets, and boats, shows and parties, dinners and affairs. Buying forgiveness or eternal gratitude on the way was a different world of many parties, functions and fashion shows cloaked as charities, foundations and good works, with the necessary fund-raising rationale and desirable tax-free status. These enabled the few "haves" to give to the many "have-nots", while having a really good time and being seen doing so, and at the same time also feeling good about it.

Not that all had bad motives in giving and partaking- it was just too easy to take advantage of those so-good do-good intentions, just like the disaster internet site scams, real donations made to fake organizations, or subscriptions to imaginary needy causes with real undisclosed and massive overhead costs. It was all about publically keeping an image of supporting "good works," keeping money in motion, and privately taking your share.

This is how he had formed connections with the church, whose influence in trying to do good crossed national and social boundaries, and brought connections to the others, the diamond traders, the oil sheiks, the rich heirs and, finally and inevitably, to the really poor. He enjoyed his work, the danger, the days spent in locations anywhere in the world, the fast pace, and the results of arresting or at least arraigning ring leaders, and those who would normally snub him, or not even know of or acknowledge his existence.

He had tried to stay honest, to be truly one of the good guys, to avoid the temptations offered and proffered: anything he wanted to change a testimony, to avoid an arrest, to ignore some evidence, to look the other way, not to take action. Indeed, that is how he had become involved in one of the greatest scams of all time.

Suddenly, his smart phone buzzed with another text message, and he tapped the screen as he walked. It seemed that Ivanovitch had been able or at least trying to talk. He was mumbling that a girl called something like "Sletvana" had tried to kill him. Farini knew he was in the ICU, or Intensive Care Unit, under police guard, being sedated and coming in and out of half-consciousness. They were still not sure if he would live, or for how long he might be semi-comatose, or even might be able to talk coherently. Both his body and his brain had been bruised and traumatized, and many bones and internals were broken. When Farini had last seen him in Florence's hospital he probably had more tubes in him than in any of the movies, and more bandage wrappings than a Frankenstein or zombie.

His many thoughts were interrupted by the crush and noise of crossing the street to the station at the end of the Viale, and set about trying to find his binario. The usual scam artists and pick pockets were hard at work, helping unwary and lost tourists find their train, their tickets or their seats, while losing their wallets, a piece of luggage or at least an unwarranted and massive tip or cash just to make some "helper" go away.

In the throng, he saw a tall person, in leopard skin top and tight, tight tights and high, high heels, who on a second closer look he recognized as a local transvestite All part of the scene and seen, he thought. After almost pushing his way through the crowds, with its luggage stacks, ticket lines, crowded benches, and people gazing at its many overhead sign boards, or trying to hear the blaring multilingual announcements above the rumbling engines, he boarded the espresso train to Rome. His reserved seat in first class was not occupied this time by any interloper asking for money just to move, or for sympathy to stay.

In his two-hour rapid journey, rushing and swaying past the country fields and the railway yards, over the bridges and the level crossings with their clanging bells, he pondered his life. He wondered if his decision was the right one, and smiled to himself about what it would or could mean.

No one would have ever connected all this, but for a strange happening.

Chapter 5

Sun, sand and sea

Life's a beach

The breeze rattled the coconut and palm tree leaves, as turquoise seas turned to foaming wavelets on the white, rippled sands. Flecks of cotton clouds scurried in lines across the views, and the sun baked glistening oiled bodies to darker hues.

"The biggest decision of the day is which beach to go to, to decide, just to decide," he said slowly, his skin darkened, his polo shirt colored, and a lilt to his voice. "Or which room to have, or lovely girl to kiss, or tourist to amuse. Eco-tour this or that they call it, the very latest trend, with the very latest price. They think they have reduced the carbon pollution- but really they have added to it!!"

Solomon Sarley laughed, loud and cheerful against the sighing sound of the sea. His gold jewelry flashed, a watch, a chain necklace, a ring.

He looked up and down the beach, wiped the heat from his brow, and offered his guest the bar seat overlooking the azure beauty of the bay and reef, where sandpipers and seagulls played, twisting lazily in the breeze and hopping along the silvered, talcum sands.

The lithely draped waitress with braids offered cool long-necked beers on special, with an extra shot.

"Here, we make money, praise the Lord. Everything is fine until it isn't. The conch are good; the weather's fine; the money flows in. Some of it is laundered, some legal, some drug trade, some investment shelters, some traded, some banks, some politicians, some wonderful scams on property, amazing inflated prices on seafront, lots and villas and of course those wealthy celebrities and entrepreneurs buying whole islands. And I mean whole islands. Praise the Lord!

"We have thousands of those to sell...big ones, little ones, lousy ones, beautiful ones, endless reefs. Name your price. You just need a plane, a boat and zillions of cash to get to them- and we control those islands too. After the Brits and the Yanks pulled out, they left us with cars driving on the wrong side of the road, abandoned satellite bases, schools with these crazy half-Scottish uniforms, a love for British tea and biscuits, our own elected politicians, and best of all free trade. All because we are freed slaves. They must have felt really, really guilty.

"So now we control the transport, imports and exports, the big cruise ships insurance, the bars, the police, the condos, the price of canned goods in the supermarket, and with the Lord's help, the drugs. The only thing we cannot control is life."

He looked up and down the beach, thoughtfully for a moment, then back to his guest, sipping his drink. "Now you have found me -so what can we control for you?"

The Agent, Clifford Hsu, felt the heat behind the question, the smile that masked a clear mind and a brutal heart. So he took a minute to think. He idly watched a few bikinis, some pale tourists, and a white yacht pass by. The waves broke on the darker waters of the reef, and then the lagoon turned to translucent blues over the sands. Life and time stood still, as the warm dampness clung to his skin and his words.

"You know Yuri introduced me to you. I understand from Yuri that you will handle it all as normal shipments - it could be disguised as just a shipment of chemicals, or fertilizer, or wood pulp, or something.....The ship will be under a Bahamas flag and carry Bahama insurance so the US and the others cannot interfere or inspect. We need you to control the shipment and the crew". He paused as the wind rattled the fronds again, and the air tasted of sea, and the fine grains of talcum sand whispered around their feet.

Yes, it was all very beautiful and he hoped he would have some time later, one day to enjoy it. But business today was business today, so he listened intently.

Money talks

Solomon had leant forward: "How much control?"

"My instructions are precise. The cargo must not arrive at its destination. Perhaps it can disappear, say, somewhere off Africa, before delivery. It should look like Moslem terrorists or drug-filled pirates. They must dump the cargo—there must be no evidence left to inspect."

"How much money?"

"You know, Solomon, not only are you wise you are greedy....and I like that. A great host, no expense spared on a beer, and straight to the key point. Money."

Solomon was just trying to extract his best deal. "I can arrange the insurance here, in a minute. All the big companies are here using our flag of convenience and enjoying our offshore tax laws. And our great rum. Even the major cyber currency exchanges are here- at least in virtual space. But it is difficult to do this disappearance and make it look real. It may be impossible."

Clifford knew he had to flatter. "If it were easy, everyone would do it. I must and do have confidence in you, Yuri told me so. The impossible just takes a little longer to achieve...look at the great discoveries, of America, of penicillin, of oil in the gulf, of the Universe expanding to its death. They all take time. So it is with the heat death of the planet, and reducing carbon emissions. And they all take money."

"How much money?"

"Solomon, you are too persistent, just drink the beer". Clifford knew he had him hooked, it was now just the price of the hook. "You get a straight fee plus a percentage...but based on performance. You can be paid in cash, in QuidCoins™, or in kind. Your choice."

Like the sea sparkles, Solomon's teeth now showed almost a snarl not a smile: "Fee? How big a fee? There are men to hire, boats to arrange, cargo to move, pirates to bribe. You talk a percentage? How many percent?"

"Say, a million, and....."

"I need five."

"Two."

"Four."

"Two and a half."

For an instant it was as if the breeze paused, the waves stood still, and the BBQ smells of fish and lobster tails wafted away. Clifford was not smiling. "We are not dealing in T-shirts from China, coral smuggled to the US, or coke running past the coastguards. We are dealing in national quotas, and in real money now, not later. You must understand, Solomon, this is a big, big deal."

Solomon smiled at the thought of his own pension fund, lying piled in a vault as cocaine bricks, gold bars, diamonds, all ready and hard substitutes for inflating notes, and backed by virtual money.

Clifford Hsu continued with the close of the sale.

"No wonder the accountants and the traders like this eco-game, and the save-the-planet folks are happy too, even with these paper reductions in emissions. Our merchant bankers are in on the deal and get a cut, as they bet on futures and trading values, so also do the owners and the major companies, EAI and CEC. Your percentage depends on performance, on completion, and will be in cash, in whatever dollars, transfers or bonds that you specify. I will tell you the amount, but only me, and I am the one and only single contact. That I control.

So, I would like to place the call that says we have a deal. Now."

The sun was going down in a glory of red clouds, shimmering seas, with the cool breeze rattling the fronds.

The seabirds circled above the sands, like vultures, and dived to pick at, and fight over the scraps amongst themselves.

Lobster tales

They both would like to enjoy the conch, champagne and lobster dinner served on white table clothes and glittering crystal on Solomon's yacht "Treasure

Island" anchored in the smart end of the marina of the Barracuda Seas Rezortz and Yacht Club©.

The decks glowed, the brass and chrome gleamed, and the lights flickered to the hum of the generator. The beat and pulse of rhythmic music surrounded the market nearby.

In his bed, he did not wear much, and the sheets felt silky, with the air conditioner singing its noisy song.

In the morning, the sun angled through the slats on the window, waking him. He luxuriated for a while, enjoying stretching and yawning, It was nearly midday when the marbled shower steamed over the mirror, which wiped clear by his towel showed a face young but old, sad but happy, wearing the empty eyes of death.

He slipped on his flowery shirt, his linen pants, and a pair of beach sneakers, the humidity making his skin feel both dry and wet at the same time.

He found her on the beach, on the stretch of sand and palms used by the tourists, just near the steps to the beach of the exclusive Barracuda Rezort. Arnika displayed her body in a bikini, near the shore and shell line, mixing in with the other sun seekers who roasted and tanned idly while sipping pina coladas from umbrellad glasses.

Her two-piece was a beautiful shade of turquoise, matching the sea, and covered enough to be respectable, but revealed just enough to be interesting. Her oiled skin was dark already, and the small scars did not show, although the slight strap tan lines added interesting and eye-catching contrasts at the edges of the fabric and across the skin. Stretched luxuriantly on her beach lounger, with a rum and coke in one hand, and a fiery novel in the other she soaked up the atmosphere, smoothed her lotion over her flesh, and luxuriated in the rays.

He squatted beside her, his fingers picking at the sand, and gazed out, as she was, at the waves lapping lazily at the white shore.

"It's a deal." His words were quick. "Solomon will do it. But only for two and a half million, plus the crew cost and the ship and insurance fees. It may all be in untraceable cyber money. He told me he had lost money on a property deal out on the West End, another failed condo-time-share or some other quick-rich real estate project with a shady consortium. So he was short of cash. I was almost in tears for him, but then he settled for less than he was asking. So we had a deal. And he gave me a great conch dinner on his yacht..."

She now knew four things. The deal was moving forward; they had a cargo; a ship; and the best of all, the money. The money complicated it, but then money was always harder to get but so much easier to spend. But what made this deal more complicated was because everyone seemed to be ready to double-cross everyone else, and that was the heart of the deal anyway.

"Does Solomon suspect anything?"

"I trust him just as much as Claudius was told by Pilate that he could trust no one. And then he was betrayed- by Pilate himself! Probably, he suspects- after all he could buy a whole luxury villa by the ocean for that money, and still have funds left over for extra drugs."

"He already has a villa by the ocean. There's a wall with razor wire that's all around it, and gold paint on the gates, a palm tree-lined driveway, guards and guns, and a different girl every night."

"Well, another deal, another day...A deal a day keeps the taxman away." He paused as his voice trailed into thoughts. "I must get back to California, before I am missed.....taxi to the airport, a quick connection through Houston. When will we meet again?"

"I don't know." Arnika sighed. "I must go to Sedona as we agreed. Once you have confirmed the China end connection, and I have Sedona closed, we are all set, and ready to go. When will you be back?"

"Next week. I will let you know."

He walked away, his heels digging in the soft sand, leaving both imprints and memories behind.

She hoped, she desired that this would all work out, that no one she liked would get hurt. Danger did not scare her, or thoughts of death. What worried her was the idea of losing friends, those who she loved, or wanted to keep forever. Her life had been always moving on, from one place to another, from one life to another, from danger to danger. Long-term friends were hard to find, even harder to keep, and good ones even more impossible to replace.

The thought that she might not see him again made her sad.

Her skin felt moist from the lotion and the heat, and it was time for lunch. The stall on the beach cooked conch and lobster tails to order, over an open barbeque, the smoke drifting over the bushes and trees that lined the shore.

The tourists came and went, the cruise ships disgorging and then swallowing their human cargo, who wandered the market place with its shaded stalls looking for souvenirs, shell necklaces, duty-free jewelry, blue-sky-and-sea postcards, pirate-faced T-shirts and made-in-China mementos.

She stretched out on the lounger by the palm trees, watching the white shapes and dark tinged rain clouds form over the land, and drift towards the beach. Her cell phone buzzed in her beach bag, and it was a text, short, simple words. It was a style she recognized.

"A. They might know where UR. Ciao."

She gathered her beach towel, sunscreen and sandals, pulled on her wispy silk turquoise coverall and hurried over the sand towards the resort steps. The first drops of rain still felt warm on her skin from the storm clouds giving up their afternoon shower. Then, like a sudden waterfall, it started pouring, silver stair rods of water splattering the sand and the leaves, as she ducked inside the entry.

It was then she saw him.

Deep breathing

He was standing to one side of the lobby beside its fountain, near the flower display of brilliant colors and spiky greenery, but directly by her path to the elevators.

Perhaps it was the way he glanced at her, perhaps the way the slightly crumpled linen jacket bulged, or the rather flashy shoes stood out, and the slightly sweaty skin, just seeming out of place in the stream and bustle of cruise ship tourists. He was slim and trim, they looked much larger and slower, with their sneakers, t-shirts, baggy shorts and one-size-fits-all wear. Arnika did not pause, did not show she had seen him, as her pulse quickened. The bikini and coverall did not give her any hiding places, so she truly felt naked.

How stupid I am, she thought, I did not think they would find me here, or try to track me down again. Not here. Not now.

What to do?

She pushed the UP button on the elevator, and with her peripheral vision could see him standing just to one side. A line, almost a crowd gathered, as the elevator took an age to come, and was full, emptying the one-nighters with their wheelies and a few business people.

The crowd pushed forward, so she let everyone get on, including the crumpled suit, and then jostling with her arms, slightly stepped back. He was trying to get out again, but there were too many people, and the doors were starting to slide shut. Quickly, she almost ran across the lobby to the stairs marked "Service only," pushed the bar opening the door, and ran down the empty concrete stairs, then stopped behind a column, looking back, holding her breath.

The door bar clanged open, and the crumpled suit ran up the stairs. Slipping off her shoes, she followed barefoot and silently, keeping back and wondering what to do next.

On the fourth and last floor, he paused. There was nowhere to hide, so where was she? Perspiring, he turned back, hurried down the stairs, looking at the steps, not seeing her just behind the column on the corner of the stairs. When he did it was too late.

Her first quick blow was aimed at the throat, with the edge of the right hand, swinging almost like a sideways sword stroke. In that instant, she thought she felt his windpipe crack. The second was a bare but bony left knee to the groin, slightly angled up for maximum impact. And pain.

"Uhhhhhh....!" was all he had to utter, as he doubled over. The final blow was a bare right knee to the face, landing perhaps slightly in front of the left ear.

As he fell sideways, she was upon him, a wraith of silk and bikini, snarling, breathing heavily. She pulled the 9mm Shield handgun from the click-holster inside his jacket, pushed it into his forehead, twisting it slightly as she pulled back the slide with her free hand.

He was gasping. His scrunched-up eyes and the blood trickle from his ear showed the pain as she bent into his face, demanding, "Who are you working for? Who are you?"

She could barely hear his whisper.

"You...you're...your..." was all she thought she could grasp among his groans and grunts. His windpipe was fractured, and blood started to bubble in his breath and foam on his lips.

"Tell me the truth! Who is it?"

His eyeballs rolled as he lapsed into unconsciousness. She rummaged through his pockets, but no badge, no wallet, just a cell phone and a scrap of folded paper. On it was written "Clifford Hsu" in block letters. So he must have seen her with him, today, this morning, perhaps on the beach.

She dragged him to a closet leading off the stairs. It was full of towels and plastic cleaner bottles, and the disposable minutiae of Rezortz™ life, shelves of shampoo and soap, coffee bags and toilet rolls.

Time to leave this beach, she thought.

Chapter 6

Vortex

The Eagle

She had flown into Page, that faraway place in the desert of Arizona. She hired a four-wheel drive luxury JK Jeep from Rezortz Rentals©, and had driven past the amazing vermillion cliffs and Lake Powell's blue water, incongruous in the desert, now full of moored house boats and surrounded by multihued cliffs.

The road twisted up to where the mesa rose like a red spire, piercing the blue sky. The land was always moving, so the main road was closed, all traffic diverted due to a landslide. It would take many years to reroute and replace, and the temporary road then stretched like an arrow, a straight line drawn into the distance as she drove across the mesa.

Down from the pueblo of houses clustered on the rocks, the worn and hand-lettered sign by the roadside said "Indian Jewelry" and "Open." A dirt track led to a small building enclosed in a lot of jangling iron, old tires and even older, paint-peeling vehicles long past their useful life.

Inside his worn and tottering shed of a building, the old storekeeper was surrounded by his displays of dolls, snakes and pots, the work of the famous Native artists and the custom silversmiths. His face was worn, but his eyes were sharp, and he extolled a welcome and launched into a monolog of the significance of the wares. He was from the Snake tribe, and admired her handbag with its faux snakeskin and silver-plated clasps. He admired her legs too, and the curve of her body in the cotton dress and the slight glisten of perspiration on her skin from the midday sun.

The Eagle kachina caught her eye, its carved wings outspread as it curved in the lurching, flying step of the Hopi dancers. It emanated a mystical story of sacred ceremonies and secret symbols, of the earth, the sky and the pueblo world.

"It's his masterwork. He is blind now and carves no more. It is made for you."

A good line for the tourists, "How much?"

The eyes sparkled some more as he studied her face. "They are all on sale. Everything is on sale: the season is ending. This one is $3000."

She sought to bargain, "How about $2000?"

He looked at her again and talked of the significance of the dances, of the vanishing culture, of the young not wanting to learn the language, of the pressure on the land to build casinos and tourist traps. "For you, $2000."

She had to buy not only the kachina, but also the silver bracelet and the bone-handled knife to both protect her and adorn her. It was a deal she could not resist, and the payment was cash. The Eagle was carved cottonwood root, painted in the delicate hues of the southwest, of cowboy and Indian country. The engraved overlay black and silver bracelet was almost a side gift in comparison. It was marked and signed by the artist. The silversmith cooperative had already dissolved as the masters died and the apprentices learned their own skills and left to sell their own work and to develop the new geometric designs. They now proudly signed their own work.

She drove down off the flat lands, with the road kill snakes which made her think of his tribe, the sights of few horses amongst the scrub and the cactus, the occasional cluster of octagonal buildings, and dirt road turn offs to the settlements, past a few rows of dried corn stalks, with the mines hiding in the distance.

She stopped at La Posada, as rest and for its great lunch in the beamed and painted room of its restored Colter buildings, adorned with eclectic art. Drove again, past the Two Arrows casino, standing like a monument in a plain near the meteor crater, like man's own mark on this barren terrain and hills.

The open road and its endless line of trucks lead down to the red rock country, to the land of the vortices, the seat of the hidden magnetic power.

This was Sedona. The one-road town, with its now grand resorts, condominiums and shopping strips lining the highway which twisted among the towering red cliffs and mounds, with names, like the Courthouse or the Bell.

Here, artists of a different age, the New Age, had gathered to seek respite from the world, inspiration in the colors, and strength from the nature. But now the rest of the world had rediscovered and found it. The place had become a tourist destination, full of red rock tours and tourists walking, the sandstone-colored houses nestled along the valley beneath the towering rocks.

She stopped at the Forest Service Center, fought through the tourist lines and found the map she was looking for of the back roads and canyons into the red rocks.

The Eagle would show her the rest of the way, and shapeshift her to safety. Or, so she hoped.

Red rock finance

The turn-off was marked on the map as a three digit dirt road, and it led up the side of the mesa and the bluff, past the dried shrubs until a vista opened of red stones, sun streaks and huge towering fluted columns of sandstone. Ages of wind and rain had sculpted their beautiful shapes and banded colors, lying at angles to the sky.

She walked out to the edge of the scenic view space, and let the breeze move her hair. She wanted to feel the vortex again, to experience the power of the mystical wind, the fields of the life force....the renewal, the mystic sense of being who you could be.

There was nothing.

But she knew there was something, and thought she heard a sound, a faint noise overhead. A hawk circled above, barely moving his wings in the thermal draft, as he turned effortlessly, swooped past the red cliffs and bid her to leave this place. There was blood on her hands, blood that matched the crimson rocks and stained the cliffs.

For her there was no turning back, no renewal. At least not now. The hawk wheeled and turned in the sky, vanishing silently, bearing its own mystery and message.

Where she was staying was a classy resort, just off the main drag that led through the town and hummed with Jeep wheels and Harley noises. It was set by the edge of the market with its fountain jets and flowers in the courtyard, with trendy cafes and galleries, away from the occult stores, the mystic readers, the four-wheeler rentals and grocery plazas.

Her room looked over the red cliffs, while the breeze sighed like a catcall under the door and raised red dust clouds in the distant view of the cliffs and buttes.

The bathroom and floors were tiled and cool, while the drapes and overhang kept out the noonday sun. She showered languorously, the water running down her breasts and thighs in shining rivulets, and then drying quickly almost without a towel at this altitude. She dressed in Western style, swirling calf length skirt, and matching open-necked turquoise shirt. The bracelet curved around her wrist showing its engraving, and the knife hidden in its sheath threaded through the belt that sparkled around her waist.

Arnika knew she had been followed, or tracked by someone. She could feel it. Her mission now was simple- to find the investment and the investors with the big money. She could handle the followers later, whoever they were.

She reflected on why she was here.

Making money had worked very well in the past in the West, with luxury resorts, golf course real estate and showy log-made ranch houses rising from the desert to tempt the greenhorns. Just sell the property, the vacation time and the ownership dream to a lucky buyer, even if they could not really afford it, using a very low rate of payment, highly leveraged and very long-term payback loan basis to cover the debt. Then package or bundle many of these loans into debt obligations, resell the package to commercial banks as assets and bonds paying interest because of the loan payments, but not as debts. Finally, to cover the risk exposure, insure these debt obligations against loss to the government bonds and commercial insurers.

Provided the property market kept going up, with inflating prices every year, everyone made money, a lot of money on paper. You could even refinance or sell your property every year tax free, and still defer the payments. If you could not afford all the property, you could buy a share- a week, a month- in the property, and trade destinations around the tourist world, where new and fancy resorts grew and prospered.

Until of course, the property market values stopped rising fast enough, and someone was still asking for their money back. When the easy money stopped flowing, the stocks fell in value, and payments became overdue, those who had borrowed more than they should could not pay. Just like an upside down Ponzi scheme, not just an asset bubble it collapsed under the inverted weight of the pyramid of bad or unpaid debt. This was the financial crisis of the world... when many banks found all they possessed were worthless or low value bad debts, unsellable property and not valuable real estate.

With Karl's insider tips, Arnika recalled, she had made her money, and got out early, without being too greedy. But some lost everything- their job, their house, their savings. Too-good-to-be-true investment schemes and payout returns turned out to be too good to be true.

Of course, the markets always recovered. Even the trendiest places, Bahamas, Florida, California, Vegas, Reno and the wild, wild West had been through that cycle before too, of boom and bust, bust and boom. And will do so again. But there were other ways to make money, to keep the billions flowing. The Internet, the web market, now enabled the latest idea not to sell property or vacation intervals, but to pre-buy membership time. Then the discounters and brokers could sell white beaches by the ocean, spa time in the mountains, and exotic island cruises, or may be a golf weekend or a tour of the Pacific, or just a trendy hotel room.

The smartest homes and galleries were lodged into the hills of red rocks and scrub, hanging onto the views, built adobe style, coral pink, tiled roofs rounded and square at the same time. As she drove up the winding, dusty red road towards the house, she thought a little more about her real target, the megalomaniac, charming, irresistible and dangerous Karl Blocheim.

Now she knew that Karl had invented some of those new and largely unregulated moneymaking schemes-his empire spread around the world, but was centered here in the vortex of money. It was neatly named Rezortz International©, and he sold dream franchises to agents who sold dream high-end, luxury resort rooms, by week, by day, by month, all using the glitzy RezortzBooking.com on the internet. The whitest beaches, the bluest skies, the largest infinity pools, the sexiest spas, in the most exclusive, desirable and expensive places on earth, the places to be, as a single, a double, a senior or a group, but always as a spender of money.

There was lots of money to be made, and Karl had indeed made a lot of it. She had known him before, and watched him gather paintings, art, sculpture, mansions and girls around him, always decorating his life. Now he decorated the red rocks with his presence, with his adobe style, pink stone colored, sprawling home, atop the mesa amid the millionaires and celebrities of "Sotheby's Ranch", as the locals called it.

The tourists even came to admire his house from afar, peaking through the wrought iron gates, or just driving in dust clouds along the walls to try to glimpse who was visiting this week.

The paparazzi also staked out the road, hoping to see some royalty, some major rock band, or just a movie star or two, perhaps taking a dip in his infinity pool, or just brazenly showing what they were worth and what a fine body they had.

Arnika could have stayed there with him. He had offered, but she knew the price of admission, and the cost of trying to exit without returning some favor or pleasure. It was all so civilized, so casual, so decadent, like his carefree, invitation-only parties that went into the late hours, and even for some breakfast and other delights in bed late into the morning.

Money talks

The study was a giant room tiled in cool Spanish fashion. The white drapes by the shutters moved in the breeze, swirling like palm tree fronds. Southwest art hung on the walls, in gorgeous array, Jd Challenger's riveting Indians, Howard Terpning's gritty cavalry, and Bev Doolittle's galloping horses. Antique guns, expensive engraved Winchesters, Sharps and Colts, with civil war swords hung between them, were stacked in rows like the arms at Hampton Court. She knew each type of weapon, had even fired a few of them, and knew their value, and also their history.

And so did he.

Karl was lounging at his desk, a baroque masterpiece of Italian inlaid walnut, with carved griffins for legs and a curved chair that matched. The desk looked familiar- she wondered from which museum, storeroom or warehouse this piece had been spirited away from. He was a little overweight, and so his designer shirt bulged out slightly where it should not, and his rolled-up colored cuffs showed a whitish skin. His face was half-turned away from her, and his profile showed extra folds beneath the chin.

 He placed his reading glasses delicately on the table, and took his eyes away from the computer screen and over to her.

"I am sorry I could not meet you at the front - but the news people and the media are watching me like hawks these days. Please, please sit down."

She draped herself on the couch near the desk- a casting couch, sinking deep in cushions of silk and endless tassels.

"Well, my dear Arnika, what a pity that you could not stay with me." His smile was almost lizard like, and his charm was like his perspiration, oozing like oil from his every pore. He eyed her up and down, and then down and up, his eyes lingering briefly but not politely on the curves and folds.

She knew what to say. "Karl, how lovely of you to ask me. But surely we must separate business from pleasure."

"What a silly idea, my dear. Why be so pure and so chaste? We could enjoy both. Perhaps we will". The charm was not a fake- he just always knew what note to hit, and what phrase to use,

Not if I have anything to say about it, she thought, now smiling too. "What a great idea! We could stay at one of your Rezortz™ places- say the one in the Bahamas."

"My friends tell me you have already been there- and that you now stay in a rival resort here in town instead of here. What kind of friend is that?" he smiled, watching her, ready to pounce.

He continued, weighing and meaning every word. "You see, I know where you stay, where everyone stays. It is all in our mega data banks- the rooms, the places, the dates, the names, the bar bills, and the extra extras. All I have to do is press a few search buttons, enter a keyword or two, or perhaps just ask my staff, and the booking computers and surveillance videos bring it all up. It's better than Homeland Security."

He waved his fingers over the screen. "You would be amazed who stays with me at my places, who politicians sleep with and who they don't, and where and how those crazy celebs spend their money..."

He waved his hand. "I know it all—or know how I can find it. My cameras, and my staff are everywhere, even where you would not believe."

Now Arnika thought she knew who might be following her. Another piece of the puzzle that perhaps now fits.

"Karl," she tried to be appealing and slightly sexy, "I want to make you an offer. I know you don't need the money, but you still need the excitement."

"Please, please, do tell me more", and he sipped his iced water, and swirled the glass a little.

So she did. About Energy Asset Inc., or EAI, and the five billion or so of ready money needed to explore the oil and gas field with the Russian Energoatomgazprom and its oligarchs and its affiliates, and the three billion for the long-term uranium rights in Africa. The fifty-fifty cut on the carbon tax with EAI. But the real prize in Europe was control of the pipelines combined with the interests of the Vatican Bank.

Then she explained how EAI would form a Joint Venture to include and enable the interest from others, in particular China Energy Corp, paying off the politicos and the officials in the process for the rights and the access to their energy market and so also their wallets.

The up-front fee needed for the set up would be balanced by a percentage of the credit value in the market at the time of delivery in the clearinghouse of the Carbon Credit Exchange.

She knew the numbers and knew he liked to know them and hear them.

"The present price was about $50 a ton, so now with the full renewable credit for nuclear and the recycling of the fuel we can get $200 million for each year, amortized over 20 years life. That's 4 billion right there. With the resulting rise in gas demand and in gas prices, all that's needed is to resell the future gas contracts, and make a killing there too. It is simply market manipulation that happens all the time, making the price fit your deal."

She paused, than added more to show she knew the scenes where he had been involved.

"You remember the gas traders in California – Enron- and the gold cartels and diamond heists. You know about the banks setting their very own interbank lending and interest rates, fiddling the exchange rates, the oil sheiks in OPEC setting production quotas, the selling of worthless collateralized debt obligations in the old real estate boom and crash, and the trading in the Euro bonds that were junk, all before the trade wars. It still goes on, it still makes money, it still pays off the politicos.

"It's not their country that gets hurt or loses elections, or devalues their Swiss account, uncovers their soft banking schemes, their inflated bit currencies, or affects their guaranteed pension funds, or the tax-free salaries in Brussels and Geneva and New York."

Arnika really knew the script. Her father would have been proud of her.

"The energy market will double or treble in the next twenty years in China, the automobiles, the nuclear power plants, the industrial parks near Hong Kong. Of course, Macau too, that will be double or bigger than Vegas, and the money will flow there, just waiting and ready to be siphoned off."

He nodded, yes, yes, yes. He was looking at her legs again for a little longer than was respectable, and at the just a little too tight fit of the blouse. She knew she needed a clincher.

"But the real prize for you, Karl, for us all, lies in China. For the energy trade and the cash flow will give you the resort access you do not have now. They are building their own massive places on the coast at Macau and hotels near the Panda reserves, not to mention the terracotta warriors. You could make a killing with the exclusive development and booking rights. All the Chinese with money are now travelling abroad- but instead of coach loads it will be just to your Rezortz^{TM}.

"You can also sell the franchises and the interval ownerships in China, and use their ghost banking and off-market credit system to move your money on and off shore. That fits with their political model of property being collectively owned, it will pay off the officials, and as an added bonus it will still keep you completely clear of US property taxes and laws."

He interrupted, leaning forward, his eyes looking at her eyes for a change. "But isn't EAI just a shell corporation, with rented office buildings in California? Another office floor in a smart building in New York City, with lots of shiny young staff? And overly expensive rent, charming receptionists and endlessly high elevators...?"

"Karl, you are right. You have seen right through to the heart of the scheme. I knew you would. Of course, it is a shell, but no more than your Rezortz International© chain- you control everything, but really you own nothing. For you it is a cash machine. A money machine."

"Flattery, my dear, will get you everything! But ..."

"Karl listen", and he did. "Your own good name need not appear here on it, even though this deal and all the money is raised through the trading system on Wall Street. It just uses the credits as collateral that we can assign to be handled by the merchant banks who bankroll EAI. The Federal Reserve, the Financial Service Authorities, the SEC and the others, they will never catch up. Some of this is being moved around in virtual QuidCoins™, so the transactions do not really exist, except in hyperspace."

She paused to see the effect of the words and the nods of agreement, then continued: "So we can make a killing. But what I really have to say and offer is off the record. It is how the deal is structured, the rights divided, the business organized and how the cash will flow."

He knew a good thing when he saw it, and she was very, very good. He smiled the lizard smile again, and then he committed. "I will have my business people look this over now, and come up with a number. 20% sounds a good round figure, for backing the five billion up front. I will want some guarantees, some protection, some warranty...." He barely paused. "But my dear, darling Arnika, all I really want is my share of you...."

Dirty work

In the bedroom, his hands were beneath her skirt immediately, feeling her flesh, slipping his fingers up her thighs to her groin. He rubbed her hard, as he kissed her shoulders, and tugged and pulled the shirt open to expose her breasts. She felt for his erect manhood, and could feel him throb and grow in her hands.

"I missed you."

"I missed you too."

"It's been so long."

"Too long.... much too long."

His tongue and hers were insistent, probing, soft, open-mouthed. As he penetrated her, she gasped a little, and felt the pulsing rise through her body as a rhythmic motion. She could feel even though she could not see. She relaxed and moaned gently as they came, together.

After, there was the long pause, not just for breath, but to hold on tightly, to feel the comfort and the caring, to feel together. To make the moment last, just a moment longer, before it too faded.

"That", she said, as a sigh, "was wonderful. With a little more practice we might even become quite good at it."

"The last time was Moscow. Remember?" He looked deeply into her eyes, and stroked her neck. "And where did you get that new scar on your back, and the bruises?"

"No, it was in Italy, and you know that was where the cut came from too. Do you want to try to trick me already?"

The folds of the sheets draped her, like casual clothing, rumpled yet wrapping the figure. His skin was soft too, and tanned, but the muscles beneath were hard. In the shadows cast into the room he seemed to her – in that instant- to be like some Roman hero carved from marble in the Vatican Museum. An Adonis, or a Perseus, or even a Gladiator.

"Did he take the bait?" Luigi almost did not want to ask, so the words were hesitatingly spoken and he watched her face carefully.

"Yes." She laughed. "And guess how much for! For his share of the five billion... not a bad start. Enough to retire from this game of catch and be caught, enough for us to hide away."

"If only we could. But there is a financial killing to do. What next?"

"A drive in the red rocks. Down into the Castle Canyon. I have some business to finish there. It might be dirty work out there in the dust and desert."

"Is anyone, someone tracking you?"

"Yes, and I don't like it."

She slowly rose and started dressing, working her way through the suitcase and the closet, picking out items on hangers, scanning them and putting some back.

The underthings were soft, lacy and flimsy, but the next layer was functional, cargo pants, an easy dry shirt unbuttoned just one too many at the cleavage, and heavy socks instead of black stockings.

"Karl seems to know about everyone and everything- or likes us to think he does. I must fix that before he tracks down the truth." Her eyes sparkled and she smiled. "Come on – get up you lazy man!!"

"You look so sexy.... so fantastic...." His bedroom eyes were on her again.

She glanced at his swelling and laughed. "Here you go again. You have your mind on only one thing, or should I say one end."

"Just one more time? For old times sake." It was almost a plea.

"Just one more time- but it will be later; and much, much later if we are dead by then. And from now on it can only be when I say. ..." He looked disappointed. "In the meantime, get your mind on something legal and not to do with screwing. Get that map out again. And where is that gun you brought for me, and the ammo?"

Luigi knew when he was beaten. Not many women ever, ever treated him this way. They usually craved for his attention. But not Arnika, who was so different in every way. He saw her beauty, her vulnerabilities, her sense of humor and her drive and need to succeed. He saw both her hard side, and her soft side, her power and her pleasure. To him, she was complete. Caught in her vortex, he had shared not just her bed, her body and her desires, but now shared her vision.

"I must call Clifford. Now," was all she said, reaching for her iPhone.

Chapter 7

Chinese puzzle

Management school

Clifford Hsu was a smooth talker. He knew it. It was his strength. It even made his career, and shaped his life.

He also knew English, Russian, Spanish and Italian as well as his native family Cantonese. Not that he had lived in China: his parents joined the flight from Hong Kong to what is known as "VanKong" in Canada when it was still an English colony, and then quickly moved down to San Francisco. There he went to school, learning about grades and drugs, and then on to Santa Bonita College in Santa Clara doing a very fashionable MBA.

Then without a pause, straight into positions working in Silicon Valley, that hectic corridor of warehouse-like offices, freeways, research parks, smart malls, university campuses, instant houses and instant fortunes. Beneath the haze in the ever-blue sky, the interstates and the BART trains were always busy, with a steady inflow of workers from all compass points and countries.

He lived mostly alone in a very smart luxury condo development in Blossom Valley near Los Gatos, or Cat City. Shadowed by pepper trees and palms, the commuters in the sound-walled freeways fed the real estate market rising at its usual crazy 20% or more a year. His friends had all been into buying and selling property using loans of other people's and bank money, so he did too. He specialized in fund and venture capital raising for the entrepreneurs who second-mortgaged their now expensive houses in the golden hills and ran start-up software ventures in rented buildings.

He fed off the creative developments shunned but still needed by the established companies. They had got big and then put big smart initials on the driveways and parking lots outside, but now had dumber technology inside their campus-like buildings. All the startups, the real innovators and computer geeks needed quick payroll cash for creating new search software engines, GUI interfaces, video games, commercial on-line websites, and smartphone apps.

He helped in the licensing of the intellectual property, the know-how, as well as the products and the endless and profitable software updates. In fact, one of the unspoken secrets of the whole software business was the continual need for updates, new versions, new apps, and quickly obsolescent operating systems. For people, like Clifford, who knew how to find the people who knew how to make new systems.

Clifford was particularly good at finding money too. Money came from the rich winery owners in the rolling hills of Napa, advances from the overpaid baseball and football sportsmen, investments from the greedy venture capital funds, funding from producers and contractors for the thriving digital animation shops, and risk capital from the venture funds who were hidden behind the giant data bases, search engines and on-line menus. There were also Foundations that wanted to do good for the environment, for the good causes.

 It all made good money too: the few shares he negotiated as security in lieu of fees in every startup easily made big returns. Major players addicted to throwing their money away always and inevitably swallowed up the new minor venture in a mega-million takeover.

Clifford was a smart cookie, who merged well into the Bay Area scene, with its rich and varied community, and its sprawling hi-tech companies, active and historical Asian trade connections, and clearly American business roots. He arranged the equity swaps and the leveraged buyouts, working with legitimate investment companies and international banks looking to manage their more shady offshore cash accounts.

He helped manage even bigger mergers and acquisitions, or M and A's, as they are known in the commercial trade, where one business was gobbled up by another. It was all about leveraged buyouts, where leveraged money was loaned to a business that could then be resold. He advised on the coincidentally restructuring of the un-repayable debts, pension funds and loans into future options and commercial paper securities. In fact, he had a long, manicured finger in many financial pies.

This financial dealing in futures was how he blundered into the energy deal business. When the open market was created in energy in California, it was easy pickings. The deals and shell dealings that companies like Enrich Energy created- and he helped them to pull off - boggled the mind. They manipulated and throttled the present and the future electricity and gas supplies, while customers paid and paid the higher prices for the privilege of living in California's sunshine and its open and largely unregulated market.

He made his salary and his bonus, and it fed his life style perfectly, that high-speed, high stakes, high payoff game of life.

"Keep the money moving," was what his boss had told him, in a moment of candor and confession, "before they find out where it has gone!"

The greening of California

Like all good things the free-for-all in energy markets had to end. He knew it had to end. It was only when energy prices really went through the roof and one morning the regulators and the politicians both woke up with the lights going out that they realized what was happening. To save the day, the electricity market prices were suddenly fixed, the power trades newly regulated, and electricity suddenly stopped being a free-for-all perishable commodity without rules.

One day his boss, clad in his usual black turtle neck, setting off his just perfectly tanned skin and with close cropped hair and rings on most of his fingers, called him aside into his office.

There, surrounded with gloss chrome and glass furniture and a panoramic view over the San Francisco Bay with its bridges, office towers and freeways, he spoke in a tense tone that partly masked his New York Jewish background.

"Clifford, you are a very smart person. I know that. We have worked together a long time, almost two years. I know that you know the scene." He paused to look out the window. "But out there things are changing fast. Almost too fast. I know you know that."

Clifford knew this was serious: his boss never talked to him about anything provided everything and everybody was making money, especially the Invisible Investors who ran the money shops in New York, Vegas, Macau and Dubai.

The boss continued his speech, as if giving one of his stock of talks or investor presentations which Clifford had mastered as the art of the deal. "Under the new regulations, emissions credits and incentives, meaning taxes on the power bills, are being introduced in ever-so-green conscious, we-must-not pollute California ....," and he explained how that meant another great opportunity and not-to-be-refused offer beckoned.

"How much is in it for me?" Clifford asked, the question both obvious and expected.

"About a million, not counting the perks, if we play this right," was the answer. "And of course, there should be a bonus, another big bonus."

So, chameleon-like, Clifford also became instantly green.

He became a financial advisor at the leading edge of the emissions market design, its bidding and the credit pricing, advising, dealing and taking a healthy fee.

When California joined with other like-minded states and provinces to share "emissions credits" and promote expensive windmills, even paying the cheaper nuclear plants to not produce or forcing them to shut down. It made more money for him, because of the free trade in energy under the three-country treaty known as NAFTA. The needed electricity to power Californian data servers, silicon chip makers and internet tablet designers now came from the Western coal plants on tribal reservations in Indian Country, from Northern power lines linked to the endless waterfalls of Canada, and from Southern gas lines that snaked across the borders from monopolies in Mexico and Texas.

And every green electron that moved made something green for Clifford. Piles and piles of green...

Hands Free

He sighed aloud into his hands-free phone in his smart new 4WD Mercedes, as he hummed along the lanes and curves of interstate 280 towards the Altos Research Park: "Please, please, not another plane trip...."

The voice on the other end was cajoling but clear, made husky velvet by its travel through cyberspace and cell towers.

"Yes, yes, Clifford, another trip, my friend. You remember, we must have the Joint Venture set up with China Energy Corp, so we, or rather EAI, can make the trades in the carbon offsets and credits. You remember that? And the ghost bank accounts to move the money?"

"Yes, Arnika", he said, "I remember. You would not let me forget...Hold on a second, the traffic demands my attention more than you do."

Clifford was distracted. As the traffic slowed and the red brake lights showed. He immediately could see an apparent accident. On the side of the freeway, a car just like his in make and color had seemingly slid off the freeway, hit a barrier, and rolled halfway onto its side. Crumpled and bent, the driver's door was crookedly open, and the whole vehicle faced the wrong way into the traffic. He could see the windshield was cracked or somehow starred strangely. There was some debris and what he thought looked like a crumpled body beside the vehicle on the dried grass.

It was the beginnings of the afternoon commute, so the other side of the freeway heading south was already heavy with traffic that now instantly backed up. All the four lanes had slowed to an untidy and shimmering crawl, as the drivers rubbernecked the scene visible across the central median.

The bougainvillea bushes in the center partly obscured their view, their bright red blooms and green leaves contrasting with the now summer-dry grass hills, and the hazy stop-start of the traffic.

As he drew nearer, he saw someone in uniform was now bending over the crumpled shape. The Highway Patrol with their black-and-white vehicles, flashing lights and gun belts were already waving at the traffic, move, move. Pass quickly.

As he sped up, he took one last, quick look. Clifford thought he had seen blood on the still shape, another fresher and brighter red bloom contrasting against a once white shirt.

He would not come back that way today, he thought.

Regaining his concentration and his speed he continued, "So I must go to China to close that part of the deal. It's just not my favorite overnight flight, with the time shift and all that hassle and hustle in Shanghai. But for you, I will do it!"

"Not just for me. For the mega-millions it will bring you."

"You think I would do this just for the money?" his indignation rising.

"Oh, Clifford. You are so cool..."

"I have just seen a terrible accident, my dear. Some one looks very dead. It could have been me. It reminds me of my mortality. So I must live before I die," he said tritely, casually.

"Clifford, you will never die. You are one of the immortals, if ever there was one...."

"Just like you?"

Without hesitation, she answered. "Yes, my dear, of course, just like me."

The greening of China

They had met just before the financial crisis, when the US and global property boom was going bust and both were looking for another way to use and not lose their money. It was at a so-called policy-makers and stakeholders conference in SFO, up on the hill at the Mark Hopkins Hotel. The topic was supposedly on energy credit portfolios, derivatives and leveraging. In the glittering ballroom, he gave an overview paper to ranks of business men, women and pundits on investment options in energy futures and the impacts of greenhouse gas limits.

His talk was well received, as far as he could tell by staring out into the sea of faces and chairs. He knew his material and the market. After all, he had helped pioneer the emissions credits system. But the promised bonus and the million had not been all as advertised. So, sadly, he left the black turtle neck, to do his own thing.

He took out a business loan, as everyone did, using his own contacts, and imagined and created an impeccable and impressive business strategic plan. He set up EAI Inc in an office building, opened a fully interactive website, and charged an outrageous consulting rate and retainer for his contract staff - and charged even more for his own time.

Everything, everything was all built on confidence, and self-confidence was something Clifford always had. He had finished his speech, gliding effortlessly as always from slide-build to slide-build, crisply emphasizing the many bullets on his slides, and still keeping to his time slot. He was confident, poised, and persuasive, perhaps a little too smooth, he wondered. He thought he had answered all the questions. He was followed on the podium by Avory Blubbins, known to Clifford and others as a self-proclaimed energy guru, having written many, many books and semi- popular articles.

Energetic and voluble, Blubbins advocated closing all the nuclear plants and covering California in wind farms and solar panels. Invest in wind, in renewable resources, whatever they may be. He had seemingly simple reasons.

First, the nukes were not needed, so why not close the plants, and plant windmills instead?

Second, windmills and solar could do it all given enough subsidies, price guarantees, and portfolio requirements.

Thirdly, all the green emission credits and money should go to windmills to help offset the needed overbuild and back up power costs since the wind was not always blowing.

Finally, no credits should go to the nuclear plants, after all they were emissions free anyway but there was always the scare of nasty radioactive wastes and Japanese-style core melt downs.

There was only a brief public Q&A, as Blubbins as usual had run over his allotted time. Clifford, now standing at the back of the room, knew it was all nonsense. After all, even though California was building nothing new, China was now building and operating about a hundred of the newest supercritical, high efficiency nuke plant designs. They used a new renewable and reusable fuel that originally came from Canada. This Chinese "nuclear rush" was simply to meet their insatiable energy demand, and to reduce the pollution and emissions due to using huge amounts of coal for powering their huge factories and new cities.

So, Clifford raised his arm, when his raised arm was recognized by the moderator on the stage to speak, he was passed the floor mike. Everyone was turning around and craning their necks to see him. Clifford simply pointed out the obvious.

"Dr Blubbins," his tongue sarcastically hung on the words, and, oh, how he loved saying that name, "Your talk is to the point. But I also must point out that credits were meant to help all emissions reductions, and so would and should reinforce using highly efficient plants. So they should not be used just subsidize politically acceptable or favorite selected ones. Why then are you advocating the opposite?"

As Blubbins waved his arms in arrogant dismissal of the remark, Clifford clearly having made his point, he slipped out of the big doors at the back of the ballroom

There and then she sought him out. His first view and his lasting vision of Arnika. Pert and pretty, in a black business pantsuit stylishly cut to suggest everything but reveal nothing, all she wanted was to ask a simple question.

Smiling, and fixing him with her beautiful and flashing eyes, she said: "That was a great talk, and a great put down. But all that crap aside, where should I put my money?"

Now when a very pretty girl asks you where to put something, you do not hesitate, not even Clifford.

"Why, with me, of course!"

So they hit it off right away, and so he helped her. They formed a business plan, and she helped him by giving him more money to invest in the credit market and the lucrative trades. It was natural team, his business flair and confidence, her money and daring, and their many, many contacts.

Soon they had a thriving business venture, and both the stakes and the rewards grew. Arnika was a silent and often absent partner, and said she had inherited money and lots of it. But they also had other shared interests besides making money: foreign travel, genuine Chinese food, sandy surf-wave beaches, driving fast on Highway 1, live theatre, and walking the fabulous de Young museum.

There was also something dangerous about her that attracted him, and others too: not just her sexy looks, but the keen mind, the sudden flash of anger in her eyes, and her fearless demeanor.

They had hatched the scheme to make many hundreds of millions together, using her connections in Europe and his in Asia. The open money exchange route used virtual currency, now called QuidCoins™, funded by some up-front money for buying influence, access and contacts in China and elsewhere, which payments were all in cash. The whole point was that the transfers and trades were not internationally traceable, and ran chaotically from account to account, seamlessly and without leaving too much of a paper trail.

"Ok. I will get on the plane from SFO tomorrow, as soon as I know that I have set up an appointment with Hwang Yang, " he paused. "Do you want to come?"

"Clifford, darling, I would love to, but I have some ugly business to finish here first in Sedona."

"I wondered where you were." The traffic was slowing again as he approached the Altos Research Park turn off. "Now I know."

She laughed, the velvet now crackling over the phone. "Not true, and not for long. Call me on the usual number when you have sealed the venture. And call me if you have not. We should meet in NYC as soon as we can. Bye, darling."

"Bye, darling." Clifford hit the End call button, and eased the car over into the right lane.

After making the turn off the freeway, two lefts and a right saw him entering the gates marked with a green colored sign for EAI Inc. There were the blank-walled and black-windowed office buildings ranked around the tree-lined car-filled parking lot, with shaded tall front doors, curved walls and mirrored glass.

The guard waved him through the gates- after all, at least on paper and while he paid the rent, this entire place was his. He drove into the parking space labeled "CEO and President only."

He smiled as he thought what a wonderful thing it was to do such a lot of good for the whole world. And at the same time make such a whole lot of easy money.

Chapter 8

Death in the afternoon

After thought

There are days that are fine, when you wake up and the world seems an amazing and lovely place and the sun and the sky beckon you to enjoy everything. Then there are the other days, the darker days. The only trouble is you never know which one it will be, she thought as she headed towards the Jeep, parked in the half shade of the oak trees and willows by the side of the lot. The sun was now streaming down as it neared mid-day, and she pulled her baseball hat just a little lower and to one side to shade her eyes.

Her life had been a wild ride, she thought, never knowing what lay around the next bend, the next sunrise, the next kiss, or the next orgasm. She remembered when she was little, her father had taught her and coached her well, to be prepared but adventurous, at the same time careful and risk taking. This life's adventure had been a risk, a major risk.

"Do it all", he had said, "But whatever you do make sure you do it well."

And he hugged her briefly but squeezing her tight, and she could feel both his caring and his concern. It was in those moments that she first truly felt love and beloved.

She touched and scrolled her iPhone to locator mode, and set the settings to data download. She threw the backpack and baseball cap onto the passenger seat. She zipped it open. The small, almost flat black 32 pistol was there, wrapped in a towel. Arnika took the handle, checked all the cylinders were loaded, and slid the safety to off. The two quick reloader magazines were there too, fully filled with fresh shells, so she stuffed those in her pant leg pockets. A quick check of the unfolded map showed the back roads marked as dashes and half lines branching off the main highways and side roads, their Forest Service numbers, and the park boundaries,

First she drove slowly, obeying the crazily low speed limit, along the divided main street, past the galleries, the magic temple-rock circle and the stores, past the malls and shops. She noticed many vehicles out now parading, some with sunroof tops, sleek Mercedes, and BMWs, and oldster vintage machines with shining paint and chrome. It always amazed her people would buy with their retirement money.

The other Jeeps were canopied with their special seats packed full of sun-screened tourists on their bouncy way to their red rock tours. Then a right turn up through a fancy housing development, with their iron gates and pink adobe walls, before a quick left turn onto a back road, with just a few exclusive houses and the state park signs.

She loved this scenery of red buttes, cactus and dried scrub, laid in an ever-spreading ever-folding red-streaked vista as she climbed up the windy half-tarmacked street. She knew she was being followed, by the way she felt shivery even in this early heat and penetrating sun. She kept an eye on the rear view, and thought she could see something. No, there were too many vehicles, but she felt uneasy and on guard.

Suddenly, the road became a dirt track, unpaved, dusty but covered in crushed red rock. The red dust rose behind her, a clear marker, and the vehicle started to bounce on the now larger rocks, so she dropped a gear into second. Now there were no more vehicles, except those behind her. Her pace slowed to ten miles an hour, bumping and swaying, the steering wheel having a mind of its own responding to the rocks, cracks and ruts. A mile seemed to take forever, forever...

It was even hotter now, the dry desert heat she knew. Feeling in the backpack, she took out the water bottle and rehydrated. Her lips and skin were dry, and the water felt like a refreshing stream as she squirted the bottle down her throat and another quick squirt down the front of her shirt between her breasts. The rivulet shone on her skin, a silver snake of coolness.

Setting the trap

The next sign showed a double track pathway into the canyon towards the top of the aptly named and shaped Castle Butte. The rocks rose pink, red and ridged in the slopes of a small canyon that became deeper and deeper as it ventured towards the butte. She turned into it, and drove about a hundred yards up the rough slope, bouncing and jerking, steering thrown from side to side. Just slightly into the canyon entrance, Arnika turned the wheels and pulled over so the driver side door was uphill and the Jeep at a slant on the slope.

She stopped the engine, and the vehicle sighed and went silent. She looked back down the trail as her own dust cleared and blew away. Sure enough, there was another dust cloud coming, perhaps about a half mile away, but the vehicle making it was still half-hidden from her by sagebrush, cactus and rocks.

Perfect, she thought.

Arnika opened the door, grabbed her gun from her backpack, pulled on her baseball cap and jumped down, placing the matt black gun on the step behind the Jeep's wheel arch. The sun burnt down, harshly.

She went to the hood, unlatched the two retainers and raised it, using the metal prop to keep it opened. A gust of hot air from the radiator and the engine blew past her. Back to pick up the gun, and a quick check of the view and the location, and then a last jet of water as she ducked down behind the driver's side wheel. She had set the trap, now, would the mice take the bait?

Peering, she could see the Cadillac making hard going of the road, slow and bouncing, with a shroud of red dust as it slowly made it up towards the turn off. It stopped by the track, and she could just see the driver's window come down and a face. The dust was gradually clearing, and through the darkened shade of the vehicle's windshield, two people were talking to each other gesturing up the hill and pointing at her vehicle.

The passenger door opened, and out stepped a man in chinos and a dull long-sleeved shirt. His sunglasses glinted briefly. He looked dark skinned and his hair was long. He looked up the trail and started to walk slowly up the hill, looking from side to side.

He was ten yards away when she rose from her crouched position, the gun in safety mode pointed down by her side, hidden, and the finger off the trigger.

"Hi!" said Arnika.

He was startled. "Hi. I didn't see you there. We just saw you stopped on the hill. Have you broken down? Are you OK? Can we help?" He mopped his brow with his forearm, and turned and waved to the Cadillac's driver to come on.

Out of the corner of her eye she saw the driver get out, but then stand behind the door one hand on the top. His other arm was down by his side, like he had something there. Likely a rifle or a shotgun she thought.

"Perhaps you can," she tried to be nonchalant. "This road was too tough for this machine, and I stalled it and killed the engine. It just kinda died."

Her finger moved to the trigger.

He smiled, so wide she could see his teeth. He was sweating from the heat and squinting behind the sunglasses against the sun. "Perhaps I can try to fix it for you. You are such a nice looking lady. I like to help nice looking ladies."

He took another few steps forward, his eyes on her, but the raised hood still half hid her. He waved back to the driver to come on again. The driver stepped out from behind the door, and started trudging up the track, but now with his right hand and arms half behind his back.

Let him get closer, she thought, or both of them. All the range and target training, all the endless field practice flooded back. Do not let them fire first. Hold the gun with two hands; do not snatch at the trigger, squeeze it and fire; watch out for the recoil. Aim and squeeze again and again. Do not hurry the shots. Do not blink. Take your time. Hit the target. Do not miss. Let the bullets do their work. Her brain was buzzing, working overtime, even in this heat, and dust.

"That would be good." Arnika laughed. "I need all the help I can get. But what the hell are you guys doing out here in a Cadillac anyway?"

The driver was now fifty feet away, still a long shot for a pistol but makeable. By her choosing, there was no cover except for some scrub bushes, dried grass and very spiky cacti.

"What's up, Carlos? What does the lady need?" he called out.

The sweating passenger called back over his shoulder. "She needs our help." He laughed. "And may be also needs something else..."

"Say please, Carlos." The driver's pace quickened, moving faster and she saw the brief outline of the vented gun barrel and its top rail. An AR15, an assault rifle.

Carlos obliged. "Please, lady, can we help you?"

"Please, and thank you," she said, trying to be alluring.

Carlos was now moving towards the Jeep. "How can you refuse us, lady? You are here all alone, out here in the desert, and here we are, two lonely guys who have everything a girl could want for help. Everything."

This sweating friend, Carlos, was now within easy range but he half hid the driver from Arnika's sight. She could see the driver was deliberately moving on the track to use Carlos as a part-shield, red dust rising from his sneakers in a small cloud.

"I might have something for you guys." She had only needed another step or two.

"No, lady. We might have something for you..." He suddenly reached behind his back with his right hand, where the holster must be.

It all happened so fast, as it always did, not in the slow, so slow choreographed motions of the movies. She was not quite sure how she fired first, but the reflexes took over as he reached back.

She brought the 32 up in her right hand, clasped it with her left hand over the right resting her forearms on the edge of the Jeep, and squeezed the trigger. The hammer rose and fell. It was not an ideal shot, too quick, the sound deafening, and the recoil kicked her hands and the gun up.

Carlos tumbled to the ground. "Ohhhh...My leg, my leg.... I'm hit, I'm hit." He continued groaning. "Lady, you shot me..."

Bad shot, she thought, as the driver brought the AR15 rifle up, moving a little to his right to try to get a clear shot. She squeezed off her second shot. It struck the dirt behind him, sending up a cloud of dust and a whine. Instantly, she corrected for the recoil kick, aimed and squeezed again.

It must have struck him somewhere high up, because he fell backwards like a lumberjack's tree, crashing to the ground and dust rising around him. The legs and feet jerked and moved a little. The canyon echoed back the gunshots like booming cannon.

Shit, she thought, I was aiming for the right gun arm. Her ears were ringing from the blasts.

Carlos was on the ground, grabbing at his leg, his gun a few feet in front of him where he had dropped it.

Her notched gun sight had his head and back in view, as he started to crawl and reach towards it.

"Don't touch it. Don't even think about it. Leave it be." Her tone alone showed she was not joking, let alone the gun. "Don't move."

"Fuck you! You shot me ....ohhh, it hurts. I'm bleeding."

"That's what a bullet will do to you. Don't move, raise your hands up so I can see them."

He raised his hands, blood and dust on one of them. His face was twisted with the pain, and sweat was everywhere. His long hair was half over his face.

"Ok, Ok, lady. You have me cold. But I need a bandage or I'll bleed to death. It hurts a lot, a real lot."

Carlos talks

Stepping out from behind the Jeep, and keeping the gun up in two hands and pointed, she was moved quickly towards Carlos. She kicked his gun, a 9mm semi-auto, to one side among the cactus and stubby dried grass. A glance showed the driver had not moved and was not moving.

"Lady, look at my leg. Please...." Carlos tried to look up at her, rolling a little to the side, and grasped at where blood stained his pant leg.

"Not in a million years." Arnika was not about to kneel down beside him to look at it or waste time.

She circled around him, still keeping the gun in two hands but now pointing down at his back. His now empty hideaway holster was on the right side of the belt of his chinos, angled and designed for quick draw. She had been right: he was a professional.

"Who are you? Who are you working for? Why did you follow me? Answer, and I'll help you. Otherwise you can just lie here and die. Slowly. Tell me the truth".

"Who the hell are you?" he shot back. "You are in real trouble now...." then winced with pain. "Just help me."

"We can play this game while you bleed to death if you want...."

"Lady, this is no game....."

She noticed him glance behind her, just a fleeting glimpse. She turned, just in time. The driver had risen to his feet, staggering, the blood running down his face, and the AR15 with its 50 shot magazine ready to aim.

She had no time to think, just time to react, to shoot twice, and now she hit him squarely in the chest. Blood spurted through his shirt,

As he fell, his finger tightened on the trigger, spraying five or six shots into the ground, pow, pow, pow, pow, pow, pow, raising the dust around him and faintly echoing. Echoes were screaming everywhere, pi-ow, pi-ow, pi-pi-ow, but she heard him grunt as he crumpled, and knew this time he was truly finished. He sprawled as he fell, an ungainly shape of arms and legs and sagebrush.

Spinning back around, she saw Carlos now trying to crawl on just two hands and one knee, dragging his wounded leg over the rough ground, towards where the gun had landed after being kicked into the cactus and grass.

The warning shot raised the dust in his face, another echo, and a shout. "Freeze! Now!!"

He did.

But six shots: empty gun. She must reload. How many times had she been told not to use all six shots?

It was the trained action, a few movements, always seeming to take too long. Tilt the gun up in her right hand, unlatch and flip open the catch with her left, the empty magazine dropping to the ground. From her pocket, the fingers of her left hand found one of the reloaders, moved it to the gun now turned upwards and by her right cheek. Push the magazine in, and pull back the barrel so the new shell filled the chamber. Then cradle her left hand under her right. Raise the gun, aim at Carlos' half-turned back. It took what seemed an age, but was over in less than five seconds.

He had seen her reload.

"Tell me what you know, damn you! And who you know."

She had little time now. No time for niceties, for cajoling, or for please and thank you's. The shots would have been heard miles away, the booms of the individual 32's, and the AR15's rattle.

"Ladeeee, please, I'm hurt. Real hurt." His voice pleading, gasping a little now, and some dust was stuck to the side of his face, the sweat cutting little clean rivulets.

"I'm not a lady, And I can hurt you more."

"Ok. Ok. Lady, I'll talk. You really killed my friend over there. I'll tell you what you want to know."

"Why did you follow me?"

He could not talk fast enough. "It was a contract. We do contract work, my poor friend, some banditos and me, down near the border. Lotsa drugs, lotsa coke, lotsa contracts. He said you owed them money or some deal you had fucked up, and you would be easy to take down, just make sure you were alone. He told us to be careful, but nothing about this shit."

He paused, almost whining, pleading, "I really need some water, Lady."

"In a minute- when we are finished. Go on."

"You headed for the red rocks and we knew you would be easy to cut off. But, Lady, we just didn't know how bad you were. Really bad."

"So? Bad is my middle name. Just tell me, who was this "he" that sent you? Who was your contract with?"

He paused.

She could sense his mind working. "How about a deal? If I tell you help me, and you let me go. Just help live, and I'll tell the cops we were ambushed. I shot myself in the leg. People do that all the time. Hell, it hurts."

No hesitation. "OK, you have a deal. I'll even give you the gun back."

He knew he was beaten and blurted out the story.

"It was a man in Laredo, near the Mexico border, not a pretty lady like you. But he had a Russian accent. Called himself Yuri. It was all in cash, $10,000 up front, in notes. Another $20,000 to follow. There are so many Russians here now, the mafia and oligarch folks, with lots of money and fingers all over the border transport business."

She knew immediately who it might be. "Yuri, eh? There are thousands of Yuri's. What else was he called? What did he look like?" She wanted to be sure.

"Yuri. That was all." He was thinking, almost out loud, really trying to recall. "Well, perhaps Yuri something Russian, like Meltsin, or Yeltsin, or Seltzer or something like that. He didn't look too good, He had a beard, a pointy beard. A real bad dude."

"Where are you going to pick up the $20,000?'

The answer surprised her. "San Francisco airport, in the Bay Area. Just drive up. We had to take a picture of your body, your nice dead body. And, as usual, a piece of your lovely ear. Just to prove it was done...." He groaned again. "Lady, I still am hurting. And still bleeding."

"Where in SFO?"

"The Airport Rezortz Hotel© parking lot, on the fourth floor."

Arnika could see the jigsaw puzzle becoming complete.

"When?"

"Just call in, let it ring- he gave us a pre-paid cellphone. It's untraceable and untrackable. The number's already in the contacts list. Just be there by 10 the next night."

Keeping him covered, she finally gave Carlos her water bottle from the Jeep, and he guzzled it down and squirted his face.

She gave him the towel to bind his leg, which he did half sitting up, tearing his pants to expose the wound. It looked fairly clean, just blood which was now congealing. The bullet looked like it had gone through the calf muscle, making a messy big hole but missing vital blood vessels. He was lucky she had hurried the shot.

Carlos was through resisting and wisecracking, just half sitting, legs outstretched in the red sand, holding his bloody leg. Keeping the 32 pointed at the back of his head, Arnika frisked him, taking his knife, his cell phone, his spare 9mm ammo clip, and his wallet.

She picked up his gun from the dirt and ejected the bullet in the chamber, flipped on the safety catch, and stuffed the muzzle into her waistband.

He limped, leg half dragging, to the Cadillac, and she told him to lie on the back seat. When Carlos had walked past the driver's angled body he barely took a look. He was used to death.

Arnika did something she usually did not do. She made a promise of help, but of course not without a sting in the tale. "I'll call for help when I am back in town. I'll just say I heard some shooting and it seemed bad. That's if no one else has called it in by now. They'll send some help.

"One more thing. If you tell them it was me, or someone remotely like me did it, I will find you. Just lie for your life, or I will kill you. I will find you and I will kill you. Wherever you are. Understand?"

Carlos nodded.

"No, actually say that you understand."

This time the words came, "I understand, lady, I understand."

In a swirl of dust she was gone. High above, a lone red tail hawk soared and circled in the sky, its wings curved like outstretched fans.

Chapter 9

Betrayal

Follow the Money

Clifford's early mentor, the turtle-necked boss, had told him always to follow the money. Now it was second nature to him, for him and by him.

He ran through the logic of their scheme in his mind again. The scheme seemed like a Chinese puzzle, seemingly simple but not easily solved. There were credits, deals, partners, a complete hall of mirrors, but with very real money. Built entirely on confidence, and using other people's money to make money, it had a neat, almost circular complexity. All they had to do was invest in something, and convince others to invest too, then their investment will give back your original investment, plus what the others have invested.

It was not really a Ponzi scheme, where the last investors' money was used to pay the first ones, but a pyramid of leveraged and insured credits, and betting against yourself on the market price.

Clifford was fascinated with it all, the daring risks, and not least the fantastic returns. He could smile to himself at their audacity and their greed.

It had all been Arnika's original idea, and for her part she provided the contacts in Russia and New York, and knew where to find the upfront funding. She provided Ivanovitch's suitcase full of money. Clifford had the entry points into China, and the access to the emissions credit markets futures markets and business structures. He provided EAI's accounts for offshore use, with a line full of "off book" credit, where people literally bet short or long on the direction of the price. It was called "hedging" and "options" in the financial trade.

The investment of five billion for uranium and thorium was made by the big players, China's Power and Energy Company and Russia's Energoatomgazprom and its affiliates. It would be offset by three billion in credits from the long-term thorium- uranium rights in Zambiosa, whose leaders were already paid off by China and Russia already for mineral rights and market access. So the import-export was easy to arrange, with a few extra envelopes full of cash to satisfy over-eager cargo inspectors and customs officials. Africa was corrupt enough anyway, with the few fat Africans taking all the wealth while the many, much thinner ones were starving. These mineral rights would be shipped virtually to a country that paid for the privilege of booking emissions credits, using the markets in EU and California.

"It's too complicated", he had told Arnika, as they sipped drinks in an elegant bar by the Embarcadero. Through full-height plate glass windows they watched the sails move like white and colored stripes across the choppy San Francisco Bay waters. Symbolically, the dark walls of Alcatraz jail beckoned across the waves.

Arnika had smiled; that devastating smile that revealed the pearly teeth and charmed the world. Gazing out of the window, she laughed.

"Clifford, that is what makes it so good. No one can track it. The money is untraceable. And no-one loses, except those we want to lose."

"We must not lose, my dear. And I have a scheme that will make it even more certain that we cannot lose."

She shifted her gaze from the Bay, back to him. "OK, what crazy deal have you thought of this time?"

"Arnika, it's easy. Just follow the money."

He explained his scheme, based on what he knew and had learnt about the trading in futures and credits.

"The money from the credits will transform into collateralized investment bonds, with the gain on the emissions credits trading transferring to my EAI Joint Venture account in New York. It's just a block from the concrete and glass canyons of Wall Street, a branch of the Vatican's IPBR held the EAI account. That account could move at a stroke of a pen a chunk of the funds to the personal accounts of Orlov and Yang, with a big percentage to me and to you, Arnika."

She was now focused and very thoughtful. The ice in the martini clinked as she idly swirled the glass, round and round.

"What about Blocheim, if he comes in with us? He is dangerous, but we need his money".

"No problem. Rest assured, Blocheim will get his investment back, plus his new opportunities in China." Clifford smiled. "Remember, to maximize the return, the ship with all the nuclear materials in it, will somehow founder. The insurers, underwriters and re-insurers would have to pay up for the lost cargo too, doubling the return on the investment. Trust me."

Arnika's smile disappeared, her gaze now straight at him. "Clifford, I trust no one. No one. Even you."

And then she laughed.

And he laughed too.

Shanghaied

His flight from San Francisco to Shanghai was the usual many hours of overnight boredom, punctuated by trying to sleep between the endless movie options, cocktails and meals of his first class cabin. In his curved body pod, with its many buttons and seat reclining positions, he could at least stretch out full length, not like the many passengers cramped and crowded into economy class at the back. No cattle transport for him.

The cabin staff were always helpful, and always smiling, and the arrival right on its morning time. He simply pulled his wheelie down from the overhead bin, was nearly first out of the plane, and wearily followed the signs to "Arrivals". The customs forms were a minor inconvenience, and passport and customs examination lines long as always. But the rows of desks for "Foreign Passports" were all manned, and the customs staff polite and efficient as always.

He could see the security cameras half hidden to look like domes in the ceiling. When beckoned, he stepped forward over the green line on the floor and handed over his passport and forms.

His chosen customs officer looked at him twice over the desk, with his passport open at the photo page, tapped something into a keyboard, and then examined the records screen carefully. Perhaps simply because of his birthplace.....

"What is your reason for being in China, Mr. Hsu? Business or pleasure?" His English was perfect.

"Business- with the China Power Company." Clifford did not hesitate, did not lie. It always paid to be honest as they likely knew already where he was staying, and probably who he was seeing. China was just like a very much more pleasant Russia. But the same rules held with officials and bureaucrats. Everyone has their role and their price.

The entry officers always began with simple questions, looking for nervous reactions not just answers. "Are you travelling with any major currency, any commercial samples, gifts or items that you will leave in China?"

"No."

"Where are you staying?"

"The Shanghai Rezortz© International Hotel."

"How long will you be here with us in China?"

"Three days at most. I leave on Friday."

"I see you have a multiple entry visa."

"Yes, I come here quite often."

Behind his counter, the officer slowly leafed through the pages of the passport, scribbled something on the form, and methodically stamped his form, his visa, and his passport, many, many times.

"Welcome again to China, Mr. Hsu," smiling and handing back the passport with both of his white-gloved hands.

Trailing his wheelie, as Clifford crossed the luggage hall with its loaded carousels of piled up luggage and cardboard boxes, and entered the "Nothing to Declare" line. The customs officer looked at his one bag, looked at him, decided he was not smuggling anything, and waved him through. He could see others who were less fortunate, with their bags unzipped on the gleaming surface of the steel table, their underwear and clothing untidily piled up, and the harassed look on their faces.

Outside the majestic new airport, shaped like a turtle's back, his car and driver were waiting, as arranged by Hwang. He was whisked along the highway, with its new condo and apartment buildings on each side, and the maglev train arcing above. Powered by invisible magnetic fields and electricity, every now and then a bullet train zipped by on its suspended rails, like a silent, sleek, but supersonic slug. Clifford preferred the safety and the personal treatment of his driver, the strong, silent type.

He was excited: this was the last cog in the wheel, the closing link, and the final deal.

As he closed his eyes that night he was thinking of the mountains of money, stacks and stacks of glistening QuidCoins^{TM}.

Tea time

The next morning, the smog was only thin and grey outside Clifford's hotel window, with the sun almost visible as a dull glow in the sky.

The key, the hidden key as Arnika had said, was China. The whole country had embarked on a massive windmill -building program, spurred on by the dreams and rhetoric of Avory Blubbins. The winds blew incessantly over the rolling, grassy plains once swept by Temujin, better known later as Genghis Khan, with his hordes and horses. Now, instead of lines of warriors, rows and rows of white propellers were whirling like massive lazy helicopters. Steel towers spiked the sky, rising at a rate of two or more a day, where once tiny circular yurts, horse leather-walled Mongolian tents, had stood for centuries. But best of all, they had the ghost banks and offshore accounts too, that could deal with EAI's account at the IPBR.

The Chinese company, China Power and Energy, he always abbreviated as CP&E, used the International Emissions Credits program to offset some of the costs of renewable wind power. The Greens had originally really set up this subsidizing funding mechanism, and the shrewd politicians had seized on it as a vote-winner and a way for them to appear at least partly "green" too. But, with great irony, CP&E used the renewable wind power credits to help bankroll its nuclear program and nuclear fuel deals, and support its energy infrastructure bribery in Africa.

Clifford was ready for his big day, the key meeting. He had put on his best dark suit, just to match all the other officials and managers he might see or be seen by.

He crossed the lobby that was all marble and chrome and vibrant artificial flowers, and here the same driver was there, patiently waiting. The offices of CP&E were not far from the Bund, that marvelous mix of old stately colonial buildings with the wondrous spires and exotic shapes of modern multi-floored office towers along the shore.

From the back seat, he could see the name China Offshore Shipping Co blazoned on the side of one huge building, the home of China's massive shipping company, COSCO. Then, behind the elegant Bund buildings, China Power and Energy was displayed on another black glass tower. There he got out. It was now a little humid, and the sun was now almost half visible, still a ghost hiding behind the smoky sky.

Going straight to the top

The elevators whisked him to the 40th floor, along with the dainty and attractive secretary with the half-slit skirt and silk blouse, whom Hwang had sent to escort him to his office from the security desk where he had signed in.

Hwang's glass-plated office overlooked the back of the Bund, and the bustling Shanghai sea promenade. Clifford remembered the expensive dinners and business meetings where he had met Hwang many times.

One of China's new elite, a party favorite and influential with good contacts everywhere, Hwang effortlessly climbed the greasy political pole to become a senior executive in CP&E responsible for international credit trading and, best of all, green programs.

He greeted Clifford warmly, shaking his hand. 'Boy, life was good' was what he thought and what he lived. He too wore a smart black suit, with a red tie, and matching black glasses. Despite his age, his hair was perfectly black, perfectly combed. His teeth perfectly white, his smile perfectly formed. Impeccable manners, courteous gestures oozed from him.

His spoken English was also perfect, though he knew Clifford knew Chinese, and knew Clifford knew he knew.

"Clifford, my friend. How good to see you. How well you look. Such a time since we met. How are you? What are you up to? How long can you stay? How was your flight?"

Clifford also knew polite small talk when he heard it. So he rattled off the required stock answers to these standard questions.

Ordering tea from his gracious assistant, Hwang invited Clifford to near the window to sit on leather couches, opposite each other. The green teas were placed and poured with elegance and skill into porcelain cups on the glass-topped table between them. Hwang waved to the assistant to leave.

Clifford knew the rules and the ropes. First praise, then the details, then the deal.

"Thank you for your hospitality, Hwang. China has such a powerful nuclear program now, the largest in the world, more new builds, more plants operating. And it is all due to you. You are the envy of the world, of everyone. And so quickly, so cheaply, so safely." The compliments poured out in a verbal waterfall.

Hwang was positively beaming with delight.

"Clifford, you are so kind. My role has been and is quite modest. We do all this for furthering the People's Republic, and for the Common Good. We have the world's largest nuclear build program, the biggest number operating, the French designs, the US designs, the Canadian designs and now we produce our own, and vastly superior designs. We digested the technology, and now we can build ours anywhere we can export, all by ourselves."

Hwang positively preened himself, full of pride at this fantastic achievement in less than twenty years.

"But as you have noticed, we do need more fuel for our reactors and for the exports. For the moment we build many, many windmills to help at home, but everyone here knows nuclear is the only answer to replace our coal and to help really clean our air. It will make us almost truly energy independent. We have to import oil and gas, and once we have digested the US fracking technology, we will have reduced that import and political cost too."

Clifford already knew the whole story. "I also know you have bought many mineral rights in Africa, including the new thorium-uranium ore for the fuel."

"Yes,' said Hwang, warming even more to his theme and to his tea. "Can I offer you a praline also? They are very good- I get them sent especially from France. No?" So he continued.

"This new fuel will help make us completely independent and self-sufficient ...eventually. No more having to buy fuel from France, the US, or Russia, our friends who try to monopolize the nuclear fuel market, and stop others from enriching and selling fuel. Canada and India helped us develop this new fuel, and we have run the technical demonstrations already.

"The fuel is known as depleted thorium-uranium in the trade, or DEPTHUR. This new fuel mix is dug up in the only known resources, and the mineral crushed, separated and processed in Zambiosa. As you might guess, the rules on contamination and use of toxic materials and waste disposal are much more flexible there than, say, in Europe or the USA. Waste and safety is not a big deal in those parts of Africa. Was it not called the Dark Continent by the old colonial powers before our time, if I remember?"

He paused. "So can you help me, Clifford, as you said you could?"

This was the real question, not just a pleasantry.

Agreement

Clifford leant forward, lowering his voice. He suspected, rightly, that the conversation was being recorded.

"What we are offering CP&E, with my partners, is a guarantee on the investment and enhanced emissions rights, on a major shipment from Africa. The proceeds will be divided between you and Russia, and my company EAI. With our friends, Russia and China, we can use the necessary options on the mineral rights to make a great deal of money."

Hwang looked up from his tea and pralines. East was indeed meeting West, a good sign. His eyes probed.

Clifford warmed to his subject. "We will help fund the fuel shipment. Under international agreements, the emissions reduction investments for the fuel would be booked in the credit trading system on Wall Street, using EAI and our brokers. Using the credits as collateral, the credits will be assigned and handled by the merchant banks, who also sold the ownership rights to EAI. The banks and the dealers had a vested interest in the success and profit of the trades as they take a percentage of the traded value, and a one-time broker fee."

Hwang was listening, and moved forward, almost spilling his tea. A slight trickle came from his lips, so Clifford could see him lick his lips, figuratively and actually.

"Clifford, my friend, this sounds too good to be true."

Clifford knew Hwang was literally already hooked, so added more. "You have not heard it all yet. The international emissions credits on the thorium-uranium futures for the fuel shipment will be tendered for sale and reinsurance by EAI, using these same banks, in the futures commodities market in New York. ..."

He paused, letting the details sink in.

"All that is needed was the price of the credit investments to be used for leverage, basically to fund the hidden bet we will make. The bet was simply called a "short sale," requiring that the value of the investment in the credits would not rise, but fall in the trading market."

"Ahhhh...." breathed Hwang, softly, suddenly seeing the beauty of the double scheme. "I see, I see. It is just like betting against future currency exchange rates. It's a bet that the credits would really fall in value. I saw such strange bets had been used by the London Whale traders, and by the banks with mortgage securities before the great Financial Crisis, basically making money by betting against themselves making money!"

"Precisely, precisely," Clifford flattered Hwang, who was pleased and now more than interested. "To make the price fall was the other, and very clever, part of the scheme. To ensure that the price would fall, the shipment of harmless and reusable thorium-uranium is of course, in good trading tradition, quite disposable.

"The shipment might even never make it to its final destination. Having moved by rail to the coast, on its way the whole cargo would simply sink somehow and completely disappear, like many ships do each year.

It could be lost in international waters while flying under a flag of convenience from, say, the Bahamas. The insurance companies would pay for that loss too, reimbursing in full the original insured value, thus providing a guarantee of the return of the whole initial investment."

"So what do you want me to do?" Hwang was impatient, eager, wiping his mouth with a napkin, and carefully setting down his cup.

"I want you to get rich. A fuel cargo of thirty thousand tons, valued at $100 per kilogram, is worth three billion on the market. We have an investor who will cover that amount, and all he wants from you in return is the hotel access rights in Macau, Beijing, Xi'an and here in Shanghai."

He paused to let it sink in, and then continued.

"I know you have the contacts to make that possible, and we can help to grease the wheels. In return, you will get a personal commission fee, a large one, payable into an offshore account in your name, or any other you may choose. We can use QuidCoins™ for the transfers, and no-one will be any the wiser."

Hwang knew he could make anything happen, especially now China had built their new islands on reefs in the Pacific. Now they controlled the sea trade despite the furor and envy of the USA.

"Clifford, I hope you do not think I would do this for any personal gain. But to further our international trade and cooperative relations, it seems highly desirable." Hwang was already mentally counting his millions. After all, others in the businesses of the New China made their piles of cash, salted away in large offshore accounts, despite the recent so-called crackdown on corruption. "What else?"

Clifford was already in the closing phase. Sensing success, he continued rapidly. "We also need you, and CP&E to talk up the value of DEPTHUR, or whatever it is called, in energy usage, safety improvements and emissions reduction. Then, the fuel shipment would be priced well above the everyday material used in all the old reactors. You are already building a hundred reactors, and completing about one every three months, so you will be believed by everyone."

Hwang smiled. "Also, as you know, Clifford, we are a recognized, designated international nuclear fuel bank. We can move whatever we need, wherever we need to. The International Nuclear Agency thinks it can inspect everything, but it is all words and agreements. We just don't tell them or disclose everything, of course. Neither does Iran, or Israel, or Pakistan. We know we can move whatever we need to under military or even commercial cover. Not even the US satellites or, how do they say, Snowdencraft can track all we do."

Clifford had a few last words. "Best of all, no one would want to salvage a potentially radioactive cargo from deep in the oceans, far from shore. We claim the full insurance value. Then, just a little later, China Power and Energy would say it's not interested in the renewable fuel any more, and was abandoning it, so the value of the future credits would completely disappear. But in the short sale market, the investment makes a guaranteed profit from the difference between the original buying price at $100 per kilogram or, say, about $50 a pound, and the new market floor price for a lost and now nearly worthless product, at a few cents per ton. We double our money again!!!"

He paused again, watching Hwang absorb the ideas, and the dollar amounts. "There is no risk. Will you do it? Are you in?"

An even longer pause, then Hwang nodded. "I agree. We must talk more privately, much more. I need the details, many more details. Join me for dinner tonight at the Bund."

Clifford knew he must make the call to Arnika, but also knew he must wait.

Chapter 10

Dead End

Carlos talks some more

Luigi felt tired: his eyelids felt heavy. To him, the cactus looked tired. For the last two nights he had not got much sleep.

The plane trip from Roma to Phoenix had taken many hours, leaving near midday, and arriving late in the afternoon. Both ways, the business class cabin had not been too full. But the connection in Washington, DC, had taken the usual three hours.

Coming into the US he had used the fast Global Entry passport line reserved for police, security, politicians and the crews. Being a cop, all his guns were let through without a problem

The afternoon temperature in Phoenix was its usual 100 plus degrees, a burning sun, and the air had that dusty dryness and hot concrete feel to his skin. The Rezortz© rental car drive to Sedona had been easy, a few hours up the freeway, and with a GPS. He fought to keep his eyes on the road, as it wavered and shimmered in the heat. Not to become too drowsy, he stopped at a roadside canopied gas station for hot coffee in a Styrofoam cup. Not exactly a cappuccino, he thought, as refreshed and awakened he piled up the last few miles. The desert cactus gave way to red rocks, corroded into fantastic cliffs, columned spires and balanced boulders.

It was just turning dusk, the blue sky turning red from the sun's last gasp at daylight, as its pink rays sank behind the buttes. "Take the first turn on the left. Arriving at address." The GPS had found the hotel. It was nestled among the rocks off the main street of Wheatville. He had texted ahead to let them know he would be there.

He did not get much sleep that night. Or the next.

Farini had had a good life, an interesting life. From his childhood in Sicily, amongst the vineyards and villas, to his early days and time in the local polizia. Through his father's many and useful connections he was offered a job in Napoli, beneath the steaming volcano of Vesuvius, in that hot bed of laundry, soccer, Pompeii ruins and garbage collection disputes. He had learnt his trade, the way to handle both criminals and politicos. And how to watch out for his own back.

He had met a lovely girl, Maria, and it was instant animal attraction and a torrid affair, with hours of delights and moments of stolen pleasure. So they married. She was a wonderful looker, a great smile, a lovely olive skin, with that swagger, swing and style only young Italian girls have, complete with the high heels and the smart talk.

But the hours of police work and the strain of just life took its toll. He had promised much, but had no time to spare and to deliver. They had separated, with both tears and tantrums, and with regret, so even now talked to each other, but both his life and hers lead in other directions.

He had worked even harder, and became known inside for his background work on the Banco Ambrosiano scandal, and the possible links to the Mafiosa, which lead him into the international crime arena.

Being in Roma, with its traffic and its magnificent Roman ruins, had brought him into contact with almost everyone who mattered, or who wielded any influence in the turmoil of Italian politics. He was sought out for assignments because of his independence, his skills, his looks and his knowledge.

That meant travel everywhere in the EU and its international financial networks. From Bruxelles to Paris, from London to Abu Dhabi, from Berlin to Buenos Aires, from Basel to New York, from Monaco to Moscow, just about from anywhere to anywhere where money laundering, scams, white-collar thefts and grand crime could be connected and where money flowed to and from.

He flew in and out of the chaotic Roma airport so regularly that the security guards and border control police there even knew him, waving him through the special entrances automatically, even giving him the access codes, and now never asked him anything, or even search him.

The same was true in London's Heathrow, in New York's Kennedy, in Paris' de Gaulle, in most of the world's main access points, where he could bypass the lines and controls as a trusted traveller too, with his iris scan, fingerprints and ID in all the international databases.

He saw how others made, or tried to make money using and moving other people's money. The leveraged bankers, the wheeler-dealer executives, the market manipulator traders, the drug carriers, all the way from the price-fixing cartels, the young make-it-now and get-out-quick entrepreneurs, the massive casino operators, the sports game gambling fixers, to the backroom agreements on false currency rate exchange agreements.

He got to know all the ways the unscrupulous tried to make crime and other innocenti pay: the grafts, the scams, the cons, the embezzlements, the fake accounts, and the pyramidal Ponzi schemes.

The Files Talk

The next morning, the sun had begun its relentless arcing in the bluest of blue skies, causing deep shadows as the crisp morning air vanished. Luigi Farini's day was already heating up as he walked into the Wheatville police station.

His face was rough and tanned, smiling, his eyes a steely blue, his handshake a vice grip. "Howdy, Inspector," greeted the detective in a turquoise, loose fitting checkered western shirt with its pocket carrying a badge, his boot-cut jeans revealing carved pointy-toed cowboy boots. An under-arm leather holster was strapped across his chest, for a right hand draw, and in it nestled a 45 semi-automatic. His words and phrases were like bullets too.

"I'm Joe Fallon. Call me Joe. Guess yaw'll made it OK. All the way from Europe, eh? Let me see your ID. That looks OK. Do come into my Office, partner. Glad you are here. Welcome to my church. Take a pew. Any pew."

There was only one, so Farini slumped into the well-worn chair with its slightly cracked plastic seat. Strewn with papers, the metal desk had a computer, a coffee mug, and a rodeo calendar. The Cowboy Cop dug into a pile of documents and produced the blue manila folder.

"Here it is," opening the file and poking a finger at a picture.

"This guy," said Joe, tilting the page towards Farini. "Carlos Ziminsky he's called - gave us a different name at first. Came in with a bullet wound in the leg. We had a call two days ago from the State Park Service folks about gunshots up in Castle Canyon. He was out there in a car, bleeding and talking about being shot, so we sent him to the hospital here. It's in our Wheatville jurisdiction, since the Park's outside the Sedona city limits."

He leafed through the sheets.

"Gave us the usual crap at first. Said he had shot himself. But the other guy at the scene was shot by a 32 and couldn't talk anymore. So we said he could be up for murder-one unless he talked. I offered him a deal: talk and we drop some the more serious charges. So he talked some, even without a lawyer. So it's not admissible evidence, but sure is crazy stuff. I thought it was all about drugs at first. But it looks more than that, and brings in your international Eurocop jurisdiction."

"What did he say?" Farini did not need the details, or the background, just the facts.

"Oh, he talked quite a lot, some crap, some real. Said he and his dead buddy had been recruited to make a hit. On a lady of all things. All they knew was they were to be told when and where to follow her. Knew she was in a Jeep. So they tailed her. She went up the Castle Canyon and they followed. But she ambushed them, took them out, and skedaddled.

"Can you believe it, they didn't even know her name. Thought it was Russian lady 'cos the guy who paid them was Russian, they thought. With a name like Ziminsky, he should know a Russian when he sees one. So we do not think he was lying on that score, even tho' he has a long RAP sheet. But who knows?"

Shrugging, Joe looked up from the sheet. "Now here's the really interesting part..."

Carlos lies

"It's already very interesting, so far, Joe. If I can call you Joe?" Farini was still trying to keep his eyes awake, but his mind buzzed with the possibilities. "OK, give me, how do you Americans say it, the scoop. Or is it the low down?"

"It's the low down here, or the 'skinny,' as I think those Brits call it." Joe the Sheriff smiled. "Ziminsky said the guy who paid for the hit was called Yuri, a Russian. He had just flown in from Moscow, they thought. Said he knew about them from his contacts in the transport business- guess that means the drug trade."

Joe was full of useful information but did not have much time for the formalities and the bureaucracies. "Now there are lots of Russians called Yuri, but not all of them fly in to the US everyday. So just as a long shot, we ran the check with what I call the Department of Homeland Insecurity, you know, the DHS. We told them we might have uncovered a terrorist or a hit man just to peak their interest and wake up their sleepy bureaucracy. So they ran their data, from Customs and Immigration, and that of their buddies at the NSA, the other security folks. It covers everything...and everybody. Who leaves, who stays, even where US citizens go, and track all their cell phone calls. Even all the calls and the sextings by the higher-ups, the politicians and the chiefs."

"No wonder some of them want to stop the call monitoring program," laughed Farini. "We have the same thing in the EuroPolice, but of course we deny that it exists. The bunga-bunga parties, the insider trading contracts, and the mafia's fixes take a lot of arranging, but we cannot let them know that we know…. Or what we know…. or how we know. Well, you know how that goes!"

Joe the Cop carried on with his briefing.

"Hey, officially, we don't know anything either. We can just deny everything. The courts can't touch what does not even exist. The doggone DHS just lets us know the answer to what we ask, not what or how they got that info. The Snowden case let people know about those other security folks, you know, the NSA, who are surveilling everybody everywhere everyday. The damn' DHS must lie in the same stable as the NSA, and are full of the same horseshit. But we don't even ask that question. Only ask the questions for which you really need to know the answers. That's the rule. Guess that's God's rule too."

He leant forward, lowering his voice: "So we can't send this info to you in any form. It, and its sources really do not exist and none of it can be used as evidence. It is real intelligence stuff, what the intel folks call humint and sigint, and real encrypted G2. Hush, hush stuff."

Luigi nodded. He knew this talk was cover phraseology for information gleaned from human agents and sources, and also from coded signal intercepts as well as clear phone records.

Seeing that nod, Joe the Cowboy continued.

 "That's why we asked you to come over here- just to see and hear this stuff yourself. Not from a local vortex or in some crystal ball. Face-to-face, mano-a-mano, so to speak. I shouldn't even really be telling you how I know. It's all about deniability, so you can and must deny you know, and so will I, partner."

Joe was thinking out loud now, letting it all hang out. "All this horseshit may violate the US Constitution and all our goddam' Rights. Some of this undercover surveillance stuff I hate too. But I have to use it – just can't tell anyone that. They'd run me straight out of town if they knew. I'm the Sheriff of Wheatville, goddammit; I need votes to stay in my job. You don't."

"Ok, what did you find? And why send for me?" Farini was now really curious. This seemingly rough cowboy really knew his work, his ground rules, and had all the right contacts.

Joe the Sheriff was turning the pages again. An expert at reading upside down, from years of such work, Luigi thought he saw the words "CLASSIFIED" printed on the heading of some of the pages. "Don't worry, greenhorn, I'll let you greenhorn look over the whole file before I put it back in the safe. Just don't make any copies. And I mean any copies of anything. You've been cleared to hear this, not to see it."

He continued, "Yuri, the DHS folks say, is in fact one Yuri Potlovski. Seems to be a real hot dude in Russia himself. He flew in from Moscow the day before. He's suspected of arranging some assassinations, and a few disappearances. He's very politically connected, works or deals with a senior government guy, a Minister called Orlov. Yuri's known to the US as being a major player or enforcer. Not to be tangled with. No, sir.

"The DHS said he was linked somehow to someone called Ivan Ivanovitch in some big money deals that went sour. Ivanovitch was a wheel in Moscow, making big bucks, but fell off the gravy train over some financial dealings. The file says it was linked to the Vatican banking scandals. You'd know more about that than I do."

Farini nodded again, letting Joe the Cop continue.

"The DHS said their sources said he had fled the country, left Russia for good. Supposed to be under some type of protection in, let me see, yes, in Italy. It was then your name came up. A big red flag. Your name, no one else's. You are tagged as the international EuroPolice guy on anything to do with Ivanovitch. It said inform you immediately. So we did. And here we are...and here you are. Welcome to Wheatville."

"Increduloso!" gasped Luigi Farini, feigning genuine astonishment. "This is all news to me despite my, as you Americans say, inside know-how. I knew about Ivanovitch, but not all this."

"Yeh, me too. So it's over to you, the Eurodicks. We can only hold Ziminsky for another day or two, charge him with some suspected minor offence, or whatever. He is coming out of hospital today sometime. His friend is less fortunate. But there are no witnesses, and we can't hold him forever. He says he was ambushed, and sure seems he was. He'll get bail. As soon as his heels hit the street,
he'll probably skip over the border anyway, and hunker down. No point in the Feds trying to extradite a small fry like him back to God's country."

"Should I talk to him?"

"If you want. But not much point. He's done his singing, and his talking. The little shit now wants his lawyer. So that's it. He knows the system.... talk just enough off the record, then deny it. The lawyer can claim inadmissibility; plus lack of evidence, and he gets off. I suggest you just read the file and enjoy. I can only give you a few minutes now."

"Anything else?" Luigi wanted to know everything he could.

"Yes, of course we tried to track down this so-called lady. Checked the hotel registers, resort bookings and daily checkouts. But lots of folks from all over are in and out of here everyday, especially out-of-towners at the weekends. Looks like she probably used a false name. Ziminsky said she was fat and blond. No one remembers anyone like that who weighs less than two or three hundred pounds. All the others are weekend trail walkers in skinny jeans. No Jeep bookings here around by a fat blond either. We just can't sit and watch video surveillance camera footage all day looking for blond ladies - the hotels and the ranch hands do that anyway."

Joe the Cowboy was now at full gallop. "We also tried to track down this Potlovski guy. He's still in our goddam' country somewhere, but we can't charge him with anything either. He is a slippery one too, from what the DHS info says. And dangerous." He tapped his gun with his left index finger. "I'd just shoot the sonofabitch if I saw him, but the law's the law. We can't even use any unfriendly persuasion any more. Ain't wasting the taxpayer's money, or any more of my time on this guy."

A tale of two stories

Then Sheriff Joe, the Cowboy Cop, paused and sighed. He carefully placed the file on the desk opposite Luigi. He got up to leave. "Excuse me, got to take a leak. Can't take the file with me. Anyway, I just don't know shit any more, but I do still know horseshit when I see it. Who really knows the truth? And who is really lying?"

"I wish I knew," replied Luigi, reaching for the file left there by Joe.

Luigi was now feeling dead tired but he leafed through the papers, and the faxes, and the e-mails.

The file had his Ziminsky's DoB, name, fingerprints, and a mug shot, dark skin, unkempt hair, and years of experience showing in the lines on his face, The file was thick with standard forms, Ziminsky's arrest and court histories, minor sentences or acquittals for this or that.

Theft- suspended sentence.

Armed robbery- three years on a plea deal and then probation.

Suspected assault- dismissed due to lack of evidence.

Assault with a deadly weapon- found not guilty as witnesses will not testify.

Possession of narcotics- found not guilty, due to false arrest without a warrant.

Good lawyers, bad crimes, faulty prosecutions. His pattern of life was a dirty trail of violence, arrests, bail and acquittals.

Lots of answers here, no questions.

He scanned through the pages once again, to make sure he knew the story. Then opened a new clipped section. Inside was the briefing note on Yuri Potlovski, labeled 'DHS Classified,' with a copy of a passport picture of the straggly beard and thin face staring out from the page. The eyes unblinking, the pupils dark. His pattern of life was shrouded in mysteries.

What was he up to?

Why was he trying to kill the girl?

If it was the girl, who was it? And what was his connection to Ivanovitch, still lying semi-comatose in an Italian hospital bed with round the clock guards? What was Orlov doing in all this? Did he know anything?

Lots of questions here, no answers.

It looked like a dead end.

"That's it. I gotta go." Joe, back from his long bathroom break, interrupted his musings. "They need me on the streets of Wheatville- there's real crime still out there. Some out-of-town yahoos making trouble —we have to keep this town real civilized. Shootings like this are real bad news. I need you to keep a low profile, real low, please. Don't talk to the press folks, they are real hungry for bad news and I don't need headlines like 'Cops helpless and clueless'."

The Cowboy Cop jangled his keys. "Must lock up this lock up. The file must go back for now. I'll be back late. You can take another look tomorrow if you want. Just give me a call."

"Can you give me the DHS or any NSA contact?"

"No way, Jose. Use your EuroPolice or whatever they're called. Come back tomorrow. You look tired. Real tired. Tireder than me. Don't know what you've bin doing all night, guy. Must be the jet lag, or the desert heat here. Get some rest, dude. Go get a drink, and get some sleep."

Waiting for Martians

The sun rose as always over the red buttes, and placed shadows by the cactus. There was a crisp chill in the air above the planet of red rocks and cliffs.

She was waiting for him, sipping coffee at a corner table inside the Martian Restaurant on the main drag. A cell phone lay on the table.

This built-in-the-fifties-and-sixties place had a curvy frontage, with rounded lines and windows. Inside, the coffee shop was heavy with chrome and decorated with lunar and Mars pictures, and stories of weird planetary aliens in the desert. The tables had old newspaper clippings under the glass tops of Nevada's famed secret Site 69, stories of eyewitness alien sightings and of alien kidnappings. The stuff of comics as well as of life.

He sat down opposite her.

"Buongiorno, caro mio. You look great," he gushed. "As always."

And she did. The natural look, casual hair, slightly tanned skin, bright eyes. Gorgeous, as always.

"There is a problem, a real problem..." she said, barely looking up, and leaving the phrase suspended in the air.

"I know."

"We have just travelled far, you and I, together but yet apart. Moscow to Italy, Bahamas and Arizona.

163

And back. We must stop meeting like this. They will suspect something. Something between us." She paused and gestured with her hands, the blue nails accentuating the tanned fingers.

"I know." Then a long pause. "I know."

"There is another problem too."

Smiling now, but questioning, his police training taking over, his mind in overdrive. "What other secrets have you not told me? Not an angry husband seeking revenge? Not another rejected lover looking for the truth?"

"Perhaps all of the above." She paused to sip the coffee. "Let the waitress know what you want for breakfast."

"I want you for breakfast."

"Not yet. Not today. Not yet."

He ordered the Western Special. What else out West but two eggs over-easy, crispy bacon, hash browns and wheat toast. And coffee in a big mug. She stayed with thin toast and decaf coffee.

Luigi was slowly relaxing, enjoying her. Arnika was relaxing too, enjoying him. It was a long time since they only had breakfast together early in the morning. Their eyes touched but their bodies did not.

Luigi dug deep into the pile of hash browns on his plate. "These are great- we don't have these in Europe."

She broke the ice first, after he had munched his way through some of the eggs and bacon, "What did you find out?"

He had a lot to tell, so much his eating stopped for a while "Lots. Yuri or someone is trying to arrange some hits here. The cops here in Wheatville, and the Feds found out that he sent some, how do they say, hired gunfolks after you. He paid them to kill."

"Hired guns," she corrected him.

"OK, Ok. But I am only supposed to get Ivanovitch's bankroll and stolen money back for the Vatican bank. Then suddenly this Yuri, the big hit man and master arranger turns up. With his very own hit men, trying to kill you. And so you shoot them, just like that. With my gun."

He was exasperated, and annoyed, but lowered his voice. "You, you are supposed to be working up some deal on emissions credits with Russia and China. Now suddenly someone is trying to kill you, and God knows who or what else. Mama mia! How did you get into this mess? How did you get me into this mess? How did we get into this mess? What have you not told me this time?"

"Well," she said, feigning innocence, "how could you say such a thing? After all, I could say you got me into this. And anyway, you wanted to be involved with me, and when that happens, my darling, you get what you want."

The hash browns were all gone, swilled down with strong, black coffee. "Americans have no idea how to make good coffee. Or how to catch you. But you have made me a criminal, a true criminal, or at least a willing accessory. I wanted you for yourself, but you

165

lead me into this...." Then a smile, "Willingly, I admit. It was so boring before you. But now so dangerous with you. Too dangerous."

Arnika knew he was under pressure, his job and her life both on the line. The danger of being caught out meeting her in exotic places, and lying about his travel. He was a great cop, a marvelous lover, a true friend, willing to bend the rules and adjust his values, and stake his life for her.

Perhaps, for once, she should tell the truth. Or at least part of the truth, enough for now.

Accomplice Confessions

"Ok. I will tell you. What I know and what I think. Just keep quiet for a minute, keep calm, and listen."

He persisted, as a policeman would.

"I want to know who you really are, what you are doing, who you are doing it with.... How I can get out of this with my life, with the money, and with you? And not end up in some jail somewhere, sharing a cell with a bunch of, how do you say, cons and conmen."

She leant forward, her arms half covering the alien faces on the tabletop.

 "I am an adventurer, as you know, so I also have lots of friends and many enemies. I have money from my dear Father, lots, plus more from what my Mother left me, plus much more made from some very risky investments and chances."

He was listening, his eyes on her eyes, so she knew he was caught in her web. "I am indeed the one who got to Ivanovitch. You knew or guessed that. He had attacked my Father, a long time ago, so I wanted to get even. Not for revenge, just to get even. He is a bad, bad person. We took his money for up-fronting the deals with China and Russia. That's the cash for the folks you know about, Orlov and Hwang, who have to be paid off in millions in offshore out-of-country accounts. In advance. We use virtual money, called QuidCoins™, you know about those. That cash is for just used for setting up the deal."

She kept going, better to tell him now, so he knew.

"But for the big killing, we needed Karl Blocheim's multi- billions to lubricate the extra-big deal on the special nuclear fuel. I know him of old, and he owes me a special favour from the past. So I have his word on that. In return Karl gets some sole franchise, licensing and casino rights in China. He loves and lives that stuff.

"Then there's Clifford, you have met him. He's the laundry man, the moneyman, managing the handling and washing the funds flowing in and out. He is setting up the off-shore shadow banking deals for China and Russia now, and setting up the credit market and insurance for the short bets in New York." Arnika sat back, watching for his reaction, nibbling at her toast, the crumbs decorating her lips.

"There, I have told you...."

Luigi looked very puzzled, and was almost thinking out loud. "Ok. It sounds to me like a scam. A big, grandioso scam. Your scam. Now, I am almost sorry that I asked you to tell me. I should arrest you. But before I do that, what about this Russian hit guy, Yuri?"

Arnika decided to tell him what she did and did not know. "I am not sure about him. I will find out. He must want it all. If he gets rid of me, and gets rid of Clifford, perhaps Yuri and Orlov think they can take over the whole deal. Or perhaps Yuri will take both his and Orlov's share and run. Either that, or he is up to something else bad we don't know about. Anyway, it's a double cross, and I trust no one...."

Then a smile, that intriguing and capturing smile.

"But you, you, my darling, have no jurisdiction here to arrest me. And, what is more..." triumphantly adding, smiling broadly, "having told you all this, you are now my accomplice!"

Farini felt both angry and sad. "In nomine Patrie! You have suckered me into this ...this...fantastic scheme. I just need Ivanovitch's money back, and nothing else. Except you, of course.... Now, I might have nothing, nothing at all, not even you...."

"You will always have me, my darling," She touched and caressed his fingers, then touched and stroked his arm. She looked lovingly, deeply into his eyes, and he melted. "I'll even get you your money, and much, much more. Millions more."

"What can I do?"

"Look, I know that Yuri is expecting to have my death reported to him soon, with a photo and my ear as evidence. In SFO, at the Rezortz© Hotel near the airport, he is to hand over $20000 in cash, the balance due to Carlos on my head. I have the phone- this phone. All I have to do is call the number. Carlos told me about it."

"Do you believe him, that Carlos guy from over the border?"

She was working it out as she went along. "Who knows? But don't worry about Carlos, he's small fry, a hired gun. Worry about Yuri. Darling, can you take care of Yuri? He's dangerous, and he's up to something. I don't know why he is in the Bay Area. Please, just find anything that will keep him out of circulation. Can you do that?"

"Yes- likely I can have him arrested on a California firearms violation, or suspected trafficking, or bringing more than $10000 in undeclared currency into the US. Or perhaps even there is even a visa technicality- the rules are so many some are always being broken. I'll have to ask the local Sheriff here to help: he knows a lot." He looked hard at her, trying to penetrate the calmness behind the beauty.

"But when do I get my money back? And when do I get you back, Arnika, when?"

"Oh, Oh..." she sighed, "now that is the real question."

Outside, somewhere in the red dust and sharp sunlight, beyond the busy tourist-filled streets, beyond the arroyos and the bluffs, the Martians perhaps had landed.

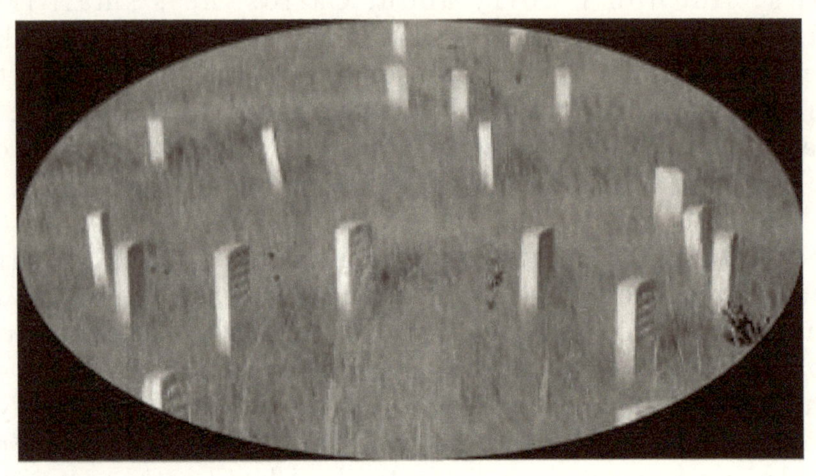

Chapter 11

Sex and the Shoot Out

Reunion

The bed was soft and warm, sheets rumpled, pillows tossed, the bedside light casting half shadows across the curved shapes and slopes of the figures lying there.

The fingers were stroking the arms, running the nails slightly over the skin, fingering and slightly scouring the front and then the back, leaving slight red lines in the flesh...

The hair curled around, in tangles, cascading, swirling, enticing, brushing the face, wrapping the neck that was so finely curved.

The body was moist, and slightly damp to the touch. There was a hazy warmth, and a lingering scent, an aroma that permeated the senses, and suffused the brain.

The breath was soft and deep, sighing almost, in a rhythmic motion that made the breasts rise and fall. Softly at first, then harder and from the throat.

The lips were soft and moist, parted then closed, revealing the pearl white teeth, and then the tongue, before curving in a smile, as the saliva glistened and broke in silver strands.

The legs curled upwards, then outwards, then together, creating pressure and release in a steady, repeated motion.

The hips moved, up and then down, up and then sideways, up, and then thrust up insistently again.

The eyes shone with pleasure, the lids closing briefly, eyelashes fluttering, then opening, the eyeballs rolling up, then back down again.

The kisses were tenderly placed tokens, but the motions were abandoned and frenetic desires.

The two bodies moved as one, sometimes slowly, sometimes quickly, entwined then separated, locked and then released. The arms wrapped behind, below, above, the touches deep and deft.

There were no words spoken except the simple ones.

"More."

"Harder."

"Hush."

"Lower."

"Higher."

"Slower."

"Softer."

"Quicker."

"Faster."

"Easy...Easy...."

"Now...now..."

"Come...Come...Come..."

"Ohhhh...Ohhhhhh.... Oooooooh...."

And so it was, time after timeless time, movement
after moving movement, breath after breathless
breath, sigh after soundless sigh.

The moment came and went so fast, the afterthoughts
remaining were only of the senses past.

The feelings, of relaxation, of comfort, of tensions
released, sweet caresses, and shared memories.

The desires were now soaked and sodden sheets, the
flimsy ecstasy now exhausted muscles, the instant
warmth now lost, the words evaporated into clouds of
silence and sighs.

A moment present, a moment past, a moment
remembered, a moment lost.

She sighed.

"It cannot last forever. Oh, why can't it last
forever...."

In the darkness is the light

Luigi slowly stroked his forehead, almost a weary
movement. He had flown up from Phoenix to San
Francisco, full of trepidation and wondering what he
was doing in the USA at all. It had been a
straightforward flight, no meals in economy class, no
free luggage, and a crowded toilet. He had called Joe
Fallon, told him he had a lead on Yuri. He asked him
to arrange for some help from the local San Mateo
Sheriff, and to cooperate with the EuroPolice.

Now perhaps he had full control of the situation, and
was about to get the Vatican funds back from Arnika.
All he had to do was go to the Airport Rezortz©

Parking Garage with the local cops and take Yuri down, as the Americans would say.

Clifford stroked his keyboard, his fingers flying. He had flown back from Shanghai to San Francisco, full of inspiration and believing the deal was now all set. The flight was easy in business class, a full recline seat, free movies, and champagne. Hwang was now on board; Orlov was on side; Blocheim had agreed the deal. He had called ahead to the dealers in New York, and the credit note issue and insured bonds were being prepared. The ship was on its way to Africa to be loaded with the new nuclear fuel. The offshore accounts and QuidCoin™ transfers would now all be arranged and done electronically from his own computer in the office. Now he had full control of the deals and the accounts, and best of all- the money. All he had to do was pick up his car from the Airport Rezortz© Parking Garage, and take the deal down.

Yuri stroked his beard incessantly, almost a nervous habit. He had been driven up from Laredo all the way to San Francisco, relaxing and dozing in the back seat of the limo, full of vodka, as the miles and the truck lights streamed past, and believing he was in sole control of the deal in Russia.

The two drivers took turns at the wheel, and they stopped every few hours for a break, a snack and to use the gas station restrooms. He had arranged for that pretty girl to be removed, the one who was taking too much share of the proceeds, and who knew far too much. That little bitch, he had been told, had attacked his old friend, Ivan Ivanovitch. He had called ahead to arrange some backup firepower. He already had removed Olga Petrova from handling and skimming any more of the accounts. His hireling used a knife to cut her fat throat in a dark street in Moscow.

True, Yuri reflected, there were still a few loose ends as the limousine swung off the freeway towards the airport.

He knew Clifford was handling the trades, and had arranged for him to be finished off on the 280N Freeway. But the idiots ID'd the wrong auto of the same make going in the wrong direction, 280S, and so they took out the wrong driver. But that was a temporary problem that could be fixed by his friends in the taxi and transport business. They would do anything for a little more cash. He knew Clifford was coming back from China……

He checked his watch- perfect timing.

"Turn here," he ordered, "Into the garage. Go to the fifth floor."

Parking fees enforced

It was a classic multistory car park, the hotel on one side of the concrete structure.

The Airport Rezortz© Parking Garage was the usual rough-walled concrete structure, with pillars, columns and stairwells and ramps of grey cement. The floors were painted with white arrows, letters and lines to tell the cars where to go and the drivers where not to. "Exit Only," "Do Not Enter," "No Parking," "Unauthorized Vehicles Will Be Towed," "No Smoking," "Turn on Headlights," "Hotel Elevator," "Display Ticket," "Pre-pay Only" all made unexciting and unwelcoming reading.

Being near the airport, and part of the hotel, guests parked at a reduced rate of just $20 a day collected at the silent half-barriers and pre-pay kiosks scattered between floors.

Banks of humming fluorescent tubes and silent LEDs lit the floors, and cast their whole unblinking stares across the parking stalls, and striped shaded regions cutting the monotony.

Video cameras tilted their one-eyed heads at the Exit and Entrance to record the comings and goings. The squeal of tires occasionally broke the silence as the autos negotiated the tight curves of the ramps and the four floors of parked vehicles.

The outside rows of cars stood in silent witness to the parade of planes as they curved into the sky, or floated in to land.

Occasionally, if a plane overran the runway, or hit the barriers on the runway's end, or entered the water surrounding this manmade causeway, the mute vehicles heard screaming sirens and the wails and hoots of the fire engines.

Yuri surveyed the scene.

Yuri had not wanted to be an enforcer, a hitman, but it made a living, and made him rich too. After a spell in the military, he was invited into the KGB, and trained in field craft and surveillance, not in intelligence gathering and profile writing. He provided cover for covert spying, tracking and protection of foreign dignitaries and scientists.

He was a big man anyway, with a real physical presence. His wife loved his muscles, his manliness and his money, and spent it on gorgeous fur hats and so-high-heeled thigh-high boots, in true Moscow style.

He had met Orlov in Moscow when, under the old regime, he was assigned to guard him for a month. Then he had accompanied him to a Party "conference" at the fleshpots of Sochi, the Party members-only resort with nightclubs. There, the favored few had access to drink, girls and special foreign currency stores. There, all the unavailable jewelry, clothes and gifts were available, and Orlov trusted him to buy what was asked, follow orders, and to see and say nothing.

So when the great Soviet Union became the former soviet union, and the free–for-all asset stripping began, he helped Orlov in enforcing more than a few deals. A varied and wonderful listing: on vodka label licenses; on oil and gas leases; on nuclear waste shipments; on burger restaurant franchises; on foreign contracts for importing reactor safety equipment. Whatever made money for the private retirement fund made sense, Orlov controlled, or knew who did.

As Orlov climbed up the greasy pole of the Kremlin power tree, so did Yuri climb. So when he wanted Olga moved out of the way because she knew too much about where the money was, and had been dipping into the accounts for her own benefit, he had been asked to "solve the problem". He had done so quickly, having a member of his bodyguard circle cut her throat on a dark street.

Now another lady was in the way, and he needed to handle and dispose of that problem too. Carlos had been referred to him as a good man, a drug lord's enforcer, who was trusted to take care of that problem.

But there was yet another problem to fix. Now all he had to do was get to the Airport Rezortz© Parking Garage and settle his debts. His phone had buzzed and showed a "missed call" from the Walmart phone number he had given to Carlos, the signal that meant the deed was done and the meeting was on.

Those guys thought they were getting paid for the hit, and so they were, in lead. A few bullets should dispose of those hired guns, making sure that they could not squeal anymore and spoil the whole deal.

Yuri's hands were clean, and all he wanted now was a quick hit to cover his tracks.

Take out Carlos, a direct Aeroflot flight to Moscow and another day of rest.

Chapter 12

Alive and Living

Living

"How lucky I am, to live here", he thought, "and what a choice."

He lived in Prague, close to the castle and Charles' Bridge. This grey stone bridge and narrow walkway with its archways and towers at each end was the link between the present and the past. Lined by statues of saints, kings and a martyrs of the Middle Ages, and leading from the Old Town of squares and celestial clocks, to the forbidding fortress on the hill. Now the castle's high walls served as the President's palace and a tourist show, its iron gates open to visit the medieval Cathedral with its glory of stained glass and vaulting ceilings.

Leaving the church behind the cathedral, with its glittering stained glass, the strains of Vivaldi's Four Seasons' echoed through his head. It was his habit to go to a concert each week, at a different majestic venue or in just a small room, where the music and the voices echoed around the walls and arches and filled the mind with sounds.

The tourists sat patiently and applauded, they streamed into the street and down the hill again towards the town and the Old Square, with its scrafittied walls of buildings adorned like ancient graffiti.

The crystal stores gleamed, the bohemian glass shone in colored blue and green rows on shelves. Souvenirs beckoned in rows of handmade and coloured nestled doll maryostras and racks of dangling marionettes. Tiny slots of Money Change shops lined the cobbled street, offering the best rates and commission-free deals for tourists.

His steps along the street were more difficult because of the throngs, and the silver handled cane he used to help support himself. Past the statues growing from the parapets, guarding the path, past the artists and jewelry stands, through the archway that lined the steep hill towards the castle.

A musician played a violin, a singer sang in a doorway, and in the main square a guitared and keyboarded band amplified its music to the passing crowds of lovely girls, T-shirted men, and the disjointed crocodiles of guided tours of Asians, Germans, Russians and curious followers.

He loved this city – its pulse, its people, its buzz and its deep and rich culture. He felt at home. His trade and business was in precious garnets, amber and high-end gems, items that could be moved without much packing, much cost and without receipts. There was always a markup, always a market, and always the challenge and fun of the deal. And the thrill of working with other dealers, of Polish, Russian and Czech origins, but crossing international borders and European rules.

This was the city of the Holy Roman Empire, always said to be neither Holy, Roman nor an Empire. The city had grown and changed even in his years there, but in a way was always unchanged, an Art Nouveau masterpiece, left largely untouched by wars, by Nazis, by Communists and by time. Even the new stores were cradled into the shells of old facades, and the new glass looked incongruous against the ornate facades, towers and arches, doorways, and the noisy, uneven but treasured cobblestones.

Life felt safe and no one knew his past, or cared to ask, and he melded with the people, invisible, accepted, incognito. This was Eastern Europe, a world that had been overrun for centuries by armies and then by tanks, where everyone had a past, a tragedy, a family history, and all knew the value of anonymity.

The coffee was Esmerelda Gisha, an exotic Panamanian blend, full of jasmine, citrus and honey flavors. A specialty of the Francouzska Restaurant, the ritzy Art Nouveau or Secession marvel of chandeliers and wall paintings, next to the magnificent façade of the Theatre and the Opera. Near here Mucha, the founder of Art Nouveau, had plied his skills of sketching the swirling forms and draped dresses, the exotic curves and flowers, which now drew the tourist crowds to his museum. He had bought Mucha's giant print of Sarah Bernhardt, and mounted it in his apartment, a tribute to both the artist and to life. Even Hitler had avoided destroying the art and the people despite the assassination of his cohorts by partisans, though an aging Mucha died after the Gestapo interrogated him for days.

He sipped the coffee, reflecting. He had taken Arnika to all of his favorite places, in the days when Russia ruled this city, and tourists were absent and restaurant menus and signs in English were few. He had had her schooled in languages, in self-defense, and in finance. Then the mighty fall of the Soviet Union had finally happened, but just like the later "Arab Spring", it turned out to be the rise of other special interests to power.

'Everything changes, but nothing changes,' he thought, 'Plus ca change, plus la meme change, how true is this saying.'

As the secret police, the old KGB, disappeared overnight to re-emerge as the new KSB, so the oligarchs gained control of the old state enterprises and monopolies. He made his money by trading with his skills at the art of the deal, helping others make killings and millions, before the actual killings started again.

He had helped Arnika get a job as a translator in the byzantine corridors of power, that took her close to and into the secret deals and meetings where money, influence and lives were traded. Here the real decisions were made as to who would gain and who would lose. Anyone could be bought, and access to those who had the power was controlled and paid for.

It was a free-for-all all that was not at all free.

Power struggle

Once the first flush of democracy and euphoria had passed, and good vodka was available, and oil and gas could be sold, the money could flow in and out. So came the rise of a new, almost tsar-like government. They did not just govern, they ruled. It was inevitable, with the power in the hands of those who knew who had the power, and where and how it could be bought.

Capitalism flourished in the hands of this few, aided by those who had retired from the secret police, but still obeyed orders and knew what was in the old files and records. If you could not be blackmailed, or coerced, you could be killed.

The major industries and assets ended up being controlled by those who knew how everything and everyone could be bought and sold. He had flourished in the chaos, not without risk moving seamlessly from power group to power group. It was not easy, both becoming rich and staying alive at the same time, but he knew he had the needed skills and the contacts. It was in that chaotic time that, as an army officer, he had met, befriended and helped Ivan, who worked for Orlov. Both were ex-KGB, ex-party members, and had excellent contacts and well-trained bodyguards. Like Yuri Potlovski.

He had helped them evade the duty and restrictions on foreign money flow, taking packages to wherever else was easy, and cash and gold and jewels were currency. Depositing the package contents in deposit accounts and safe boxes was easy for transfer to Switzerland or the Bahamas or the big banks. In those days, the banking secrecy meant no taxes, no records and no worry about the value of the ruble, or whatever became of the Euro currency exchange rates.

But he knew too much, knew who was making and taking the secret deals, who owed what to who, and importantly where it all was hidden. The millions stashed in his accounts were no match for their billions and zillions stashed in Zurich, or invested in London real estate, in oil and gas ventures, and in soccer clubs.

He had nearly finished his coffee. It tasted great.
He pulled out his cell phone and started to sweep the screens, looking for the latest messages and alerts.

He had wanted out of the scene in Russia, it was too dangerous, the warning signals were clear. No one kept their power or their money forever. If you were an out of favor oil and gas gazillionaire you flocked to London before the assassins flocked to you, or moved to some Italian villa, just to hide out of sight.

He knew at least they would not try the method again that was used in London. They killed a guy called Litvinenko by putting a highly radioactive poison in his and his colleagues Ceylon tea at a so-called business meeting. Luckily, his colleague vomited that night, but unluckily for him Litvinenko did not throw up. So he died a slow death in agony as his bone marrow and blood cells died. Cellular apoptosis, they called the living death in the fancy medical jargon. But that devious method of radiation poisoning, although clever and fatal, was too obviously statecraft, and the contamination too easily traceable. It was 'statecraft,' that polite word for getting away with murder.

He was wary, but not scared, as he prepared to leave the country, He knew the threat was there and growing.

But what would they use? And who would try? And where? Well, he had found that out in Istanbul.

A Friend

"Hello, my friend."

"I wondered if you would make it on time, Justin," and he smiled and looked up from his phone, having just tapped out his latest note. "Coffee? Beer? Czech liqueur?"

"How about a handshake first, and then a draft pilsner..."

They shook hands. His friend was young. As was the style, a slight unshaven beard covered his thin face, and he wore a loose fitting T-shirt and jeans. The designer logos were what mattered, He carried a cell phone at his waist and a smile on his lips.

They ordered the beer and another special coffee. Both arrived with a flourish and a receipt.

"Where is she?" his first question.

"I should perhaps not tell you, if she has not told you. But as far as I know, in the USA."

"She has been gone so long, and did not tell me," clearly pained at not knowing and not being told.

"Look, Justin. I owe you something but not everything. As Jan's son, the son of one of my best friends, I have helped you. Ok, you have fallen for my daughter. Many have. I do not run her life, and she does not tell me everything about hers. It is up to her to tell you what she wants to tell you."

"Why is she there? Why not tell me?"

"You know her life is not, how can I say, usual. Or normal. She spends time here, there, in California, in Russia, in Europe, everywhere. It is the modern way. Your life is not usual either, a painter, an artist, an actor and now a media celebrity." He paused, and sipped the coffee and watched his face and the sincerity of his concern. "Listen. I talk to you as I would a son- let her be who and what and where she wants to be."

"You are the only one she listens too. The only one she trusts." Now the words were stronger. "She says she cares for me, but how do I know?"

"Aaaaahhh... that is the question, and with Arnika you may never know."

"If you let me know where she is or maybe, I will go and find her. I want to find her"

"Justin, so do many people. Many people."

"But I love her."

"So do many people...."

Justin was now desperate, and getting angrier. His voice trembled. "I would give everything for her.... you must understand. You must help."

He wanted to help, but knew it was a risk. Justin was in love, naïve, more money and fame than sense. Infatuated, and impatient. As many were, he was still thinking that social media and high speed downloads reflected reality, and that life was just a series of electronic conversations.

"Listen carefully. Go to the Bahamas. Ask for Soloman Sarley, down by the marketplace. Say you are looking for Clifford Hsu who was working a deal with him. Use your wits and status, tell him Clifford is your business manager. He does that job for Arnika. Then Soloman may be able to help you. But only if you pay him. He loves money, and I mean loves money. But, Justin, do not tell the police or anyone about anything, or about Clifford. Her life is complicated enough without having anyone else but you looking for her!"

Justin was amazed, again. "Clifford? I don't know anything about him either! She said she only told me about you as a special favor, and so that you would know me. And she said the same thing- do not tell anyone about you!!" He looked down and then simply shook his head, "I don't understand why...."

All he could say was, "Think not why, Justin, think how. Have another beer- sometimes in life that is the only answer. As you drink it, I will tell you a little more about what to say. And what not to do."

So he did.

The wisdom of Soloman

It was a long flight. From artsy Prague to the crowded duty-free areas of Heathrow, connecting then on to even more crowded and humid Miami. Standing in endless lines for customs and DHS questions, photos and fingerprints, no transit permits allowed even with just carry-on bags.

Then a taxi to Fort Lauderdale, the center for all-inclusive package cruises on gigantic white-painted floating hotel ships to the Caribbean islands and their sandy beaches in the quest for touristic paradise. Then a slow ferry to the island carving through the turquoise sea, to stand in line for more customs clearances, and then buy some fine rum at low, low prices from a duty-free store and a much more laid back atmosphere.

Soloman was not hard to find. Everyone on the island knew him. How his daughters had all the fast-food franchises, and he had the shipping rights that kept prices high and the wages low. How he owned most of the markets too- everyone still had to eat. But he was known to be generous to those who needed help.

But he was harder to get to see. So Justin worked on his celebrity status. He sent a social media message about how he was looking for investors for a new movie to be set and shot in the Bahamas. It would be a kind of James Bond or Secret Agent plot, with lots of bikini and muscle appeal. It worked.

Soloman's office was high in a hotel wing above the beach, near the casino. A penthouse suite, with much glass, endless views of the harbor and the curving sands, lots of chrome and many faux leather chairs, the walls with black flat screens, the floors with ornate tiling and the doors each with a bodyguard in at least XXL size.

Soloman greeted Justin with a wave of his hand to sit down and also settled into a chair.

"Have a drink, a Bahama Mama. I'll pour." And he did. Then a question, "So, you are here to make a movie?" His smile was full of teeth, like a shark's.

"Yes, and no."

"No?" He looked puzzled.

"Well, I need to get some information too. So if I get that info everything else, and the movie and the money follows." He was sweating slightly– the time shift, the travel even in first class, and the humidity, all added to the strain.

"Money? How much money?" Soloman could not resist the lure.

Justin knew just about enough about the business to appear and sound plausible.

"A production shoot here is about 20 million, plus the stars time and fees, insurance and the overheads like transport, lodging, food. You get a major cut or a percentage. My Business Manager takes care of all of that. He is called Clifford Hsu. You know him."

Soloman was leaning forward, a body language that expressed interest. "Yes, I know him. But not about making movies."

Justin feigned he knew, after all his whole image was of a smart celeb. He could sing, he could dance, he could act, he could smile for a selfie.

"He does lots of deals, and I don't know all of them. He just handles my stuff. But he has gone missing on me, so we need to track him down. He said he was coming this way- I thought it was about the movie. Do you know where he is – is he still here?"

Soloman sensed a problem, and it both sounded and smelt bad. "I can't track him down for you- but I hope he is not using your money to pay me for some other deal!! If so he is just shark bait. It wouldn't be just the tourists who would love to see that jaws show... the feeding frenzy down by the harbor."

"I hope so too. Where is he?"

"He left me his cell number and business card...but you should know this anyway."

Justin thought quickly.

"I did. But his office does not answer, just a message. So I texted him. When he did not reply, I wondered if he was stuck here- sometimes the connections are not good or the sim cards on the phones do not work. So I came. I wanted to meet you anyway." That at least was partly true.

Soloman smiled and rifled through a drawer in his desk, and pulled out the business card. "Here is what he gave me – but I also need a small down payment on the movie."

The rest of his long day was just arranging the down payment in US cash. His real business manager could handle that transfer. Justin had an unlimited debit card, and a PIN number, and an e-pay account. The payment had to be a little less than $10000 at a time to avoid the international money transfer reporting limits. That is what he told Soloman, who gladly accepted this as a small financial consideration, or advisory fee, or consultancy contract, or retainer. In return, he promised his undying support for the movie, plus any help in finding Clifford.

Soloman did not know that with his wisdom, and Justin did not know that with his simple act they had possibly blown apart the entire deal for the boat. The card read:

Clifford Hsu

**President and CEO
EAI Inc,
2300 Altos Research Park,
Altos, CA 93404**

Hsu101@EAIInc.com

Turning it over, scrawled in pen characters was a handwritten phone number.

It was all Justin needed, plus of course a burger and fries and a first-class plane ticket to San Francisco that came through on his smartphone. While he was in 'Frisco, his manager and handlers could put out his usual social media messages, and as usual no one would know it was not really him, or where he was going. A driver would meet him with a limousine at the airport arrivals doors, and as cover he would wear his usual dark glasses and tattered jeans.

He could stay at the International Rezortz© Hotel near the airport as he usually did, as they always gave him the President's suite on the top floor. He loved the king-sized bed, marbled shower and separate jet tub, a fully stocked bar, deep-cushioned couches, private concierge, and best of all his very own super-speed gigabyte-download Wi-Fi link.

"Fame has its merits," he smiled to himself.

After all, he could not know that was precisely where everyone else was also heading.

Chapter 13

The Last Woman Standing

Luigi checks out the fourth floor

In his very long and checkered career, Luigi had been in on many busts and arrests, but not in a US parking garage. This one worried him. Too public, too many floors to cover, no hidden stake-out positions, no single choke points because of entrances and exits at all sides; and obstacles in the firing lines, concrete columns and parked cars, low ceilings and even lower lighting.

He drove slowly up the spiral ramps, 1, 2, 3 to the fourth level and pulled into a free space labeled F4 H37 on the pillar. In one glance he saw the ways in, and the ways out, the best spots for an ambush, the distance to the exits, and the people flow. Lines of parked autos, and the silence broken by the rumble of an occasional person hauling a wheeled set of luggage, followed by the quick whine of a starter motor.

Why am I here, he wondered.

It was not just the money, and the megadeals. Of all the different places he could have been, a coffee shop sipping cappuccino, a hotel room with Arnika, a restaurant by the Rialto Bridge with Arnika. "Oh, Arnika, where are you?" the words ran through his head. He tried to focus without much success, to put aside his daydreaming, and his yearning. Because, truth to tell, he was worried. 'Concentrate,' he muttered to himself, 'concentrate...'

His thoughts still wandered, here and there. What he really wanted, he reminded himself, was to get the money back for the Vatican, so he could have that promised statue that reminded him so much of her, only her, all of her....

Another hitch in police coordination: the promised San Mateo police contact had not arrived. Luigi's rental car was unmarked, and so he could not block off the parking garage escape routes just by himself. He had tried phoning the central dispatcher as he drove up, and was told someone was definitely on the way but the commuting traffic on the 101 Freeway was snarled up by an accident. All six lanes south were moving at a crawl or less for about four miles out of the city.

He had not wanted to involve the airport police, as they were much too visibly armed and uniformed. They were OK for warning off terrorists looking for a soft target or small-time pickpockets looking for a quick bag snatch. But activating them would be a too public show of force, a display of firepower and numbers that would really warn off a professional like Yuri.

Now even Luigi's cell phone would not work underground with the concrete and steel all around. All the signal bars on the flat screen showed grey with no strength, and the phone was "no service." He was on his own, as usual.

The plan was simple: just find Yuri and try to arrest him. If he resisted, in any way, shoot him, preferably in the head, but certainly fatally. If not, provoke him so he would try to run, or pull a gun, or drive off. No warning shot, no "Stop, police!" or "Hands up!", no conversation.

Carlos limps to the fourth floor.

He was not happy. His leg hurt. Worse still, his pride hurt.

Carlos was indeed a proud man, of his work, his beautiful family, his sheer survival. He had prospered while many had ended up buried in the sand of Mexican beaches, or lying pegged out in a desert somewhere, or gunned down in the street, or lost deep into hard drug use.

He had not betrayed anyone, cut a dirty deal, or double-crossed his boss, or skimmed the drug money. They moved packages across the border using people who carried the loads, literally *las mulas*, the dispensable pack mules. Those who survived the border crossing could then run free as illegals, get a job on a lettuce or potato farm, and apply for this or that amnesty and driving license, or just surrender and be deported again. Carlos would sometimes give them a few dollars extra to buy a bus ticket, new shoes, or their silence.

I am an honest criminal, a trusted man, he reassured himself. My trade is drugs and my loyalty is protecting the cartel. His boss, *El Jefe* Juan Sanchez, the cartel's kingpin, knew the Russian connection, and how they provided money to help finance, bribe and protect the trade. When *El Jefe* hired him out to do a job, he did it, no questions, no fuss, no mess.

But, this time, just this time, Yuri had misled them. He had paid for a simple service, for a favor, without letting it be known what they were really up against. He had called it a simple hit, on a lone woman. Not an ambush by some gun-toting, smart lady. Even the $10000 cash deposited up front with another $30000 promised and due on delivery of a suitably severed ear lobe was not enough. Yuri, whoever, must think they are stupid. He must pay with his life.

After getting out of Wheatville's jail free, Carlos had bought another cheap cellphone and talked to *El Jefe*, giving him the story of the ambush. When Juan heard about it he was pretty *loco* mad too. Yuri had indicated it was a simple job, and that all he needed was the cover Juan gave that it would appear to be the usual drug deal gone bad. But they had lost a good man, *un miembro y companero muy respestado en la banda*, with a value much greater than Yuri's paltry fee.

And Carlos' pride really hurt more than his leg.

"What should I do, chief?" Carlos had asked. "I want to get that smart lady who shot me, and that Ruski dude who lied. Muerto, dead, dead, dead...."

The short reply was colored with a cool anger. "Carlos, *mi amigo*, make him pay. Leave the girl for now – we target her later. Get our dinero and collect the debt for the dead before he leaves town," was all Juan said. Then, "I will activate some of our friends to help you in San Francisco. And then come home."

It was the only OK that Carlos needed. Plus the friends, three of them from East Side San Jose, who turned up in San Mateo with fancy clothes and even fancier weapons, 9mms, semi-autos, and a trunk full of loaded magazines, and a handful of passports for him to choose a new border crossing identity.

Plus a bottle of tequila.

So here they all were, heading to the fourth floor of the garage. The long guns were under their long coats, the short pistols in holsters. Plus a razor knife for cutting the ear. The concrete was hard beneath their sneakers, with every step jarring Carlos' wound.

Yuri should be there with the cash, waiting.

The plan was simple.

Carlos would approach Yuri on his own, ask for the money, and as soon as Carlos gave the signal by dipping into a brown paper package, the sidemen would open up.

Then take the money and run, or in his case limp, to the car. Head south towards San Diego where Juan had a stash house, a 10,000 square feet Spanish-style villa in the foothills, he could rest up there, let his leg heal a little. And then cross the border at their usual place when the police heat was gone.

Yuri takes position on the fourth floor

Yuri looked at the chosen spot, just a few meters from the doors of the hotel elevator.

There was no other quick way out.

He knew where to position firepower. He made his two men cover the Exits. Yuri Konstantinovich Petlovski had been trained in the command and support of "militarized firing units," meaning armored tanks and rocket launchers. He had also been trained to position his own strikes to kill, quickly, not just from a distance but close up and personal.

His lovely wife was also from Moscow, and he had positioned them and their three children in a smart apartment close to the ring road. Located near the crowded metro, with its splendid and baroque architecture, myriads of signs and subterranean corridors with their endless streams and clitter-clatter of people, all burrowing below the clogged roads and dangerous crossings. He could commute to the office in just ten minutes, a privilege few Moscovites enjoyed or could afford.

He was a person of few words. But like many, he smoked a little and drank a little more, liked the nightclubs and the assignments, the money and the deals. They took him to the drug king's palaces, suppliers in Afghanistan, Iraq, Oregon and Mexico, to the glitzy pads of distributors in Vegas, New York and Florida.

For the oil and gas energy deals, to soaring skyscraper headquarters and marble-tiled hotels, in Dubai, Houston, Calgary, Qatar, as well as in Moscow.

For the banking accounts and transfers, London, Rome, the Bahamas, Caymans, Beijing and Zurich literally beckoned for business. His passports had so many stamps, visas and added page inserts they were like a tour book telling a story of where, when and how long.

He was known as a fixer and knew the authorities had a big file on him. But he kept his own hands clean and never carried too much cash, guns or packages himself. For the Litvinenko radiation poisoning hit, he had used a couple of ex-TSB contacts, set up the cover story and spirited them out of London to Moscow, where there is no possible extradition. Their trail led back to Russia, but it did not matter- the UK and the Euro police issued warrants but were literally unarresting. They were fed impressive looking testimonies and officially recorded statements. For the Vatican bank official too, it was easy to make it look like a simple suicide hanging himself from a bridge.

"Take care of this lady, Yuri," was what Orlov had said. "We must get our hands on the money."

And suddenly, the temptation became too much. The millions and zillions could all be his, with no more worries than how to spend it all.

Yuri's plan was simple. Offer Carlos the package of fake notes in exchange for the ear lobe, and then take him down. Then a quick trip down the freeway to Altos to extract Hsu. Persuade him to release the secret account numbers needed to e-move the funds, and tell Yuri where the girl was. Simple questions, needing simple answers.

Some persuasion would be necessary, maybe a few hits with a sneaker inside a sports sock to the more delicate and sensitive parts of Hsu's body. The parts he really wanted to keep intact. Or some intricate metal rod and knife work that hurts but does not kill, and just rearranges his features a little.

Then for Yuri a short overnight flight to London, where his wife would be waiting, thinking it was all just for a little vacation arranged so he could also watch a Premier League soccer match. He liked watching the international star players perform in the Bundesliga, La Liga and especially the Premier League matches, all in HD on his big screen. Now he could see them in person from a box, and drink a little vodka at the same time.

Blocheim's view of the fourth floor

Karl had thought carefully about the deal that Arnika offered, along with all her other desirable assets she had openly displayed, as always. About the few billions needed to explore the oil and gas fields with Energoatomgazprom and the other few billion for the long-term uranium rights in Africa. The fifty-fifty cut on the carbon tax, the interest in the pipelines and the Vatican Bank, were all deal sweeteners on the side. Nice to have, but not necessary.

They could have all that risk.

But the link to China Energy Corp, and the payoff with Chinese hotel rights would indeed make him the biggest wheel there. It was simply too good a market opportunity.

He leveraged some of his assets, took a loan against some Rezortz© stock, most of which he owned, and paid Arnika the upfront funding, via Clifford Hsu, with a guarantee clause.

So he needed to keep a close watch of this guy, Hsu. Up early in Sedona, he just entered his name and company into his search-and-find system. He scanned for the telltale tracks left by credit cards, car rentals, bar bills, gas stations, reservations, hotel stays, internet searches, downloads and connections made on International Rezortz© free Wi-Fi and www.rezortzmail.com mail, and the updates on his social media and professional links.

On the screens up came Hsu's travels to Moscow and Shanghai. He had stayed one night at the SFO airport International Rezortz© Hotel in a 1BR King Bed suite for $350 a night, and paid $60 a day to park his expensive 4WD Mercedes for a few days, using the valet service. A quick camera scan and walk through by the security staff confirmed it was parked in the "Valet Parking Only" area, on the corner of the fourth floor. He had just left Shanghai, but had not booked another room night in SFO, so must be going on somewhere.

As was usual, Karl made very sure his surveillance staff covered that space. An e-tracking tag was placed underneath the rear fender - just in case of theft, he told his staff.

The plan was simple. Track Hsu. It was all so easy. He could track Senators being indiscreet, big celebs behaving badly like celebrities, and local politicians receiving freebie rooms and flights. People now had to disclose so much about themselves when on the booking websites; and even told more and more about themselves on social media pages. Karl made sure the information and data he gathered were securely filed, password-protected and firewalled, encrypted and not downloadable.

He could track Justin, the celeb, knew that he had been seeing Arnika. He knew they met by chance at his points-only Rezortz© condominium complex in Hawaii, where he made a fortune every day just having his on-site presentation staff selling at crazy prices to the guests.

Strangely, Justin was coming into SFO later that evening by himself, on a transatlantic flight booked through the last-minute discount listings at RezortzFlights©. It made Karl wonder where she was staying: sometimes even he could not find her.

The last man standing

The gray shadow became a figure, limping towards him.

"Hi, Yuri. I have what you wanted."

The voice echoed around the space. He peered towards the figure, and in the half-light felt he saw another figure behind him by a few cars.

"Who's that with you, Carlos?"

"Amigo, it's my amigo, my driver. I have a wounded leg, and I need a driver." He was just a few cars away. "We had to park on the next deck, and walk down. That ladeee you sent me to find, she shot me before I shot her, the bitch."

Yuri smiled to himself- she must have been good. "Where's the evidence?"

"In here," and Carlos held up a brown paper bag, a grocery supermarket bag, crinkled and with 'SuperFoods' in curly big letters. "I'll show you..." He started to put his hand in the bag.

"Throw the bag over to me."

"Hey, you can trust me, Yuri."

It happened quickly, too quickly. Carlos stepped sideways behind the nearest car, a shiny Lincoln with an even shinier hood. The figure behind Carlos raised his AR15 semi-automatic, and opened up at Yuri. A half- silenced rapid low pow-pow-pow-pow-pow, the small 223 bullets literally pinging off the metal and plastic autos behind Yuri.

Yuri felt something strike him in the side– lucky he was as usual wearing an armored vest. Uncomfortable, a tight fit, and too hot, but it worked. He grunted with the impact, dropped to one knee, bringing his 9mm up. Too late. From over the Lincoln's hood came the short boom of Carlos' 45, a big six-gun with a big shell, and an even bigger recoil. He had a clear shot: with no silencer, it echoed and re-echoed.

The 45 bullet was a home defense snub-nose dum-dum type, available at any good gun store in the Western USA. Because he was kneeling, it hit Yuri in the lower thigh below his vest, plowing and ripping through his flesh, flaring out like a mushroom. As it struck his hipbone it disintegrated into pieces designed to make maximum damage, sending fragments into muscle and sinew. The impact was awful. Blood and skin flew in pieces as he fell backwards, screaming, dropping the 9mm pistol.

From the other end of the garage, Luigi had seen this limping man, who he did not know, talking to someone. Moving towards someone, someone half-hidden from Luigi by a column. The limping man and his someone spoke few inaudible words, then suddenly the rattle of the first three, four, five shots. Luigi ducked behind the nearest car, not knowing if they were aiming at him. The boom of the 45 and the scream were clear enough.

Luigi reached for his cell phone: still no signal. He raised himself up to look. Carlos was now leaning over the hood as his companion sprayed more bullets towards where Yuri, still half-hidden, was now a bloody mess on the floor.

But Luigi had given away his position to Carlos's other sideman, who half saw the movement. He shouted something to Carlos, and opened up with a new pow-pow-pow, the bullets skimming so closely past Luigi that he thought he felt the draft and heard the quick whine.

Carlos thought right away this must be one of Yuri's men. He could see that Yuri was finished, lying groaning and his face in a grimace of pain, clutching his thigh.

His gesture and wave was to his three companions, his backup and sidemen, to move on Luigi.

Carlos half ducked, half ran towards Yuri, keeping as low as he could. He knelt awkwardly angled beside him, his own damaged leg only half bent. Yuri tried to reach for the gun on the now bloody concrete floor, so Carlos stuck the barrel of the 45 in his face. He could see that Yuri's jacket was peppered with holes, but all the shots had hit the vest except one that had pierced his right arm near the wrist.

"You, my amigo, are a dead amigo."

"Why?" he gasped.

"Because you owe. Give me the money. Then I might let you live."

Yuri rolled back, and tried to pull open his jacket. Carlos pulled the white envelope from Yuri's breast pocket. It had a bullet hole in it, but no blood. He ripped it open, tearing with his free hand nothing but blank sheets of paper.

He tossed the papers aside, "You double-crossing sonofabitch. Where, where is my $50000?"

Yuri was in pain from the damage to his thigh and groin. In shock, he was turning grey and his hands, legs and lips starting to quiver and shake uncontrollably. His hands were clawed. Carlos levered himself up using his free arm on the car, carefully pointed the gun and squeezed the trigger.

Behind them, behind the rows of parked cars, more shots, more muffled pow-pow-pows. Then the bark of a 32, then more shots.

On the runway nearby, another jet swooped in to land, its engines screaming.

Chapter 14

Island fever

Shooting the breeze

The airport was humming, as ever. Everyone had a connection to make- to the splendors of Europe, the mysteries of Asia, the politics of Washington, or just the lure of Hawaii.

That is where she had been before, on Kauai, the Garden Island, a land of forever breezes, swaying palms, old cane fields, strutting cockerels with feathered fantails and pecking hens by the roadside. How she loved the laid back living, the sense of timelessness, the tidy untidiness, and the endless breaking of the ocean waves.

The hills and mountains were wrapped in swaths of green jungle, and streaked by the white ribbons of water cascades. Here, the old families, the descendants of early missionaries or sugar cane planters, owned almost all the land.

Now also the remainder paid for by the nouveau riche of California's Silicon Valley, who had tweeted and messaged their way to billions, or by this-or-that hotel corporation, like Rezort International©. So that the tourists could wander the surf swept beaches and the old villages, with their T-shirt shops, burger palaces or high-end restaurants and art galleries. For the valued visitors, these shaded stores specialized in floor to ceiling exotic scenes, of jungles, palm trees, waterfalls or flowers, bright colors and blooms, and sometimes of the bygone days, earthy tones and red sunsets. By "local" artists: some were good, some bad, some expensive, some cheap.

Those cliff tops were where she had stayed, enjoying the staggering views of the jagged coast and chasms of Napili, and the endless waves swept onto the sandy beach in the curving bay of Hanalei. The resorts clung to the cliffs of Princeville, gazing windows towards the mysterious and always misty jagged green edges of the north shore.

She knew the people here, these old families who had survived the early days and the later land rush. They had made the hotels and resorts stay below the height of a palm tree, and only leased out the land but not sold it. That way they had kept the heritage and the calm, despite having to make a living from ice cream and adventure tours, and real estate deals, and helicopter tours of the amazing stream-riven green-clothed mountains. The past lingered, overshadowing the present.

She could have a bought a piece of this paradise, a condo by the endless beaches with fountains and tennis courts and torch lights. Or the isolation and peace of a cottage in the hill up a red dirt road hiding from the world. But she was here on business. After all her old friend owned many time shares and management contracts, and was leasing and fleecing the tourists.

So she could stay anywhere in splendor that she wanted, and he would provide both a bed and protection of a kind never thought of before.

Anonymity.

Bright sun, drizzle, heavy rain in shower sheets, the air humid and forever warm. If the weather was not good where she was on one side of the island, she just drove round the only road to another beach shielded from the rain and clouds. The rain on her skin was a warm caress, a refreshing damp, then gone, evaporated by the trade winds forever blowing through her hair and her life. How she loved it. It touched her soul, and wrapped her life in calm and warmth.

"We have been so many places, you and I." His words floated across the patio like the puffy white clouds in the breeze, interrupting her reverie.

He had just flown into Lihue on a nonstop from LA, and had not even been able to change into a Hawaiian shirt and shorts. "And done and seen so many things. Think of the money made and lost, the big wheels risking their cash just to make another few dollars. Think of those oil and gas guys drilling everywhere, even the Arctic, and the human waste being thrown into the oceans, and into the power plant tips and garbage dumps. And here we are in this paradise."

She sighed, brought back to reality again and the demands of real life. "It's been great, and I wish we all learned something. I should have started a corporation called "Make-a-Buck Inc." There would have been a lot of investors!"

She paused. "We are using the whole Planet like one giant roulette wheel, betting on the many outcomes, and hoping to win in the short term while knowing we will lose in the end."

"Well, we did make a buck, or two... we made our bets, and now even Karl is happy with his Rezortz resorts deal."

"Ha! A zillion bucks or two! A zillion zillion. But we may have lost one good friend...." her voice tailed off. It was hard to forget, to set aside in her mind the passion, the pleasure, the person, the love, the promises made, and the promises failed. A tear formed, for a moment, clouding her eye. She faltered, then regained her equilibrium and her calm.

"Tell me about it- at least what I should know. What happened exactly?"

It was not easy

It was not complicated.

"You don't know all of this stuff because I thought it best you did not know. But now, now you must know. It's not easy to talk about some of this," and she paused.

He nodded in understanding. "I know. I know. Just tell me what I need to know."

"Ok. Luigi told me he was going to take out Yuri, if he could. He went to SFO, the airport, to take him out legally with help from the local Polizia, so we would be safe from the Russian mob, Orlov's hit men. You know Orlov, the one who had sent gunmen after me. But it all went wrong for them."

She was not sure how much to reveal.

"Anyway, I had left the second hitman alive, and that was my big, big mistake. He was more of a professional than I knew, and must have had more cartel contacts than the FBI and DHS combined- and as many assault rifles."

She paused to brush her hair back and take a sip of the pina colada, and to brush aside the tear. Then went on.

"Karl called me and told me what he had seen, what had happened – he had most of it on his videos and screens, and anyway it happened on one of his properties. You know the scene."

"Yeah," He smiled. "I had my car there, and the whole place was all cordoned off. I couldn't even get into the garage. I had to take a limo home from the airport."

She was not happy. "So the word from Karl is that Yuri was taken down by the cartel hitman, and then they saw Luigi was there. He was no match for their firepower. He's still in the hospital. He might not live. He's been shot three or four times. They don't know if he will pull through. I didn't try to contact him at all; there are just too many looking after him, and a huge media scrum waiting for news."

She felt a little better just by talking about it.

"It's a laugh a minute. They now say he is quite a hero, a brave Eurocop taking on the whole drug scene and showing up the local police. They say the cops did not turn up to help until it was too late, perhaps because someone somewhere had been paid or warned off, and that someone had been told it was wiser for them not to get involved. And that is likely true. Or not. I don't know." She thought for a moment, and the warm breeze swept over her skin again. "I don't know who knows...."

She listened to the breeze rattling the palms. "That's about it. That's my story. What is your story?"

He wanted a shower, a nice dinner for Mahi Mahi, and an air conditioner. He tried to be brief.

"You know the other deals all went through Ok. It was not easy. We have our billions and Karl has the promises for his China Rezortz© rights. It's a new virtual room-night and casino corporation that he will have in a Joint Venture with my friends in China. The

212

shipment is still in transit but not yet sunk, but everything else that is our part is secure."

"You are a genius!"

"Maybe! Now, I might even be able to retire!" He allowed himself a smile. "A little early, perhaps buy a ranch or a big house here overlooking the ocean. Why not, it's only ten million or so. And then I can live just midway between Silicon Valley and Shanghai. What will you do, Arnika?"

She felt a little more relaxed, which is what Hawaii does to you if you let it. "No long-term plans for me. Oh, I'll give Father a call, and let him know I'm alive and OK. He worries so."

Then a real smile, the lips parting, the teeth glistening. "Then go meet my Celeb friend. He is literally dying to see me, and has followed me across the world, all the way here. He's over at the Grand Kauai Rezortz© place, in a huge, huge suite. He's asked me over for drinks, dinner, and whatever...."

"Well," Clifford laughed. "When he called me, I did tell him you were coming to Hawaii! What do you see in him?"

She laughed. "He may need my protection from his fans. And perhaps also some fun, excitement, danger, and- most of all perhaps me...."

The dating game

She strolled through the lobby, towards the gardens where the torch flames flickered and smoked along

213

the path. The restaurant ahead with its palm leaf roof was surrounded by rivers and lakes filled with huge coy, gliding and sliding.

The sunset quietly as a golden orb casting a red glare and glow over the surf breaking on the reefs. The jagged shapes of the waving palm leaves cut long, long shadows on the sand, where the guests had spent their lazy days laid out on the towels and loungers.

In this warmth, she wore the cloth as if sprayed onto her flesh, so tight that every fold and crease of the dress revealed the moves and strides she made beneath. The straps on the sandals were thin and colored, to show off painted toenails. The cloth that wrapped the skin was frothy, just like her laughter.

Beneath, she wore little at all, the cloth designed to bare the skin, to seduce the eyes and entrap the hands. Thin straps of lace, thin wisps of silk, thinly disguised the body beneath....

Thousands of miles away a man struggled to survive.

And even further, in the hills, a solitary hawk soared and swirled in the thermals, a speck with curved wings and eyes that missed nothing below....

215